---------------- ★ ----------------

IT WAS OVER SO QUICKLY STELLA COULD HARDLY BELIEVE IT.

George's head and arms were visible. He was trying to extricate himself from the freezing water, but he could get no purchase on the slippery surface. His eyes lifted wildly to Roy and went past him to Stella. The pleading look died and was replaced by comprehension. Then Roy put a boot on his shoulder and pushed; George slipped beneath the surface, his accusing eyes burning into her.

FRIGOR MORTIS

---------------- ★ ----------------

McInerny's "characters are all delightfully entertaining."

—*Publishers Weekly*

"McInerny is a tantalizing storyteller who weaves together the separate narrative threads and builds suspense to a slam-bang shootout."

—*Washington Post Book World*

D0035419

FRIGOR MORTIS

RALPH McINERNY

WORLDWIDE®

TORONTO · NEW YORK · LONDON · PARIS
AMSTERDAM · STOCKHOLM · HAMBURG
ATHENS · MILAN · TOKYO · SYDNEY

Richard Wilbur's poem, "A Shallot," is from *The Mind-Reader*, copyright © 1976 by Richard Wilbur. Reprinted by permission of Harcourt Brace Jovanovich.

FRIGOR MORTIS

A Worldwide Mystery/September 1991

This edition is reprinted by arrangement with Atheneum Publishers, an imprint of Macmillan Publishing Company.

ISBN 0-373-26080-6

For Mary and Tom Hosford

ONE

THE HOUSE was half a mile east of town on a two-lane road that clung to the contours of the land, rising and falling with the peaks and valleys, a continuous double yellow line down its center because there was never enough view of the road ahead to make passing safe. There was only one small sign posted, the same height as the mailbox and very easy to miss. NICODEMUS USED BOOKS. You almost had to know the bookstore was there in order to find it, as though business were tolerated rather than sought.

If you saw the sign and slowed in time to make the turn, a gravel drive led you past the house to a parking area big enough to accommodate three cars. The bookstore, a large metal structure, a modified version of a prefab farm building, was behind the two-car garage. The walkway along the fence protecting the swimming pool took the customer to it. In the window of the door another sign. OPEN.

The building had been erected on a large rectangular concrete slab, and after you entered, setting off the little bell mounted overhead, an aisle the width of the door drew the eye between stacks of books to the open area where the proprietor Steve Nicodemus, bearded, bald, smoking a pipe, sat with his feet in an opened lower drawer of his desk, a book on his lap, a cat asleep on the couch opposite.

If an activity is work only if you'd rather be doing something else, Steve Nicodemus was not working, even though the store was open, it being a Wednesday—he opened from ten to six Monday, Wednesday, and Friday—but in principle he could be disturbed at any time. At the moment, there was one person perusing the books. Corbett, a gangly myopic dentist on his day off, had been in the Civil War section for the past hour. Corbett would eventually buy something, he always did, but not for some time yet, so Nicodemus lovingly turned the pages of Trollope's two-volume *Life of Cicero*, a recent acquisition, rare to the point of inaccessibility. Its value was variously quoted but always at many times what Nicodemus had paid for it.

Perhaps some social scientist has produced a profile of those who go into the used book trade, but it was Nicodemus's experience from attendance at local and midwestern meetings that most of his competitors were as unlikely as himself.

As a marine noncom stationed at El Toro in California, Nicodemus had become acquainted with the base library when he first visited the PX. Getting a transfer to the library from his squadron had been one of his finest feats as a clerk, and the fact that he himself had been the beneficiary made it all the sweeter. The time was October 1945; he was eighteen years old, the war was over, the corps was in chaos, since almost no one remembered what the peacetime marines was like. It was not combat he was fleeing but the boredom of weeks spent awaiting orders that simply shifted men from one casual squadron to another. No wonder men grumbled that the war was over—not those who had seen it, of course, only those who had enlisted with visions of island warfare dancing in their heads and were now wasting away their youth lying in temporary quarters.

Nicodemus spent the better part of his enlistment in the library, a flunky job, but he didn't aspire to any title or responsibility; he just wanted to be where the books were. That was when he read his way through American literature.

At the time he had vague thoughts of becoming a writer, and he pored over the lives of Hemingway and Dos Passos and Fitzgerald as if he were reading of future friends. He decided that he wouldn't go to college when he got out of the corps. A writer needs little formal education. That was the theory he developed reading about Hemingway and O'Hara and James T. Farrell. Best to see the world, acquire the experience out of which writing would come. And read, of course, read constantly, read everything.

The reading left little time for writing, and with the passage of time the idea of writing slipped away. The books already in existence captivated him. His love for their contents spread to the books themselves and he became knowledgeable about editions, publishers, rare books. On weekend passes he visited used bookstores in Los Angeles and Santa Monica, even went up to Frisco several times. He began to buy a few books. More important, he came to know what books he wanted eventually to buy.

He was discharged from Great Lakes, that being the marine or naval station closest to his home. When he walked through the gate and onto the highway he was still wearing his uniform and carrying a duffel bag but he knew a chapter of his life was ending. The duffel bag was more unwieldy than heavy. His books had been shipped home from California in boxes. He thumbed his way across southern Wisconsin to La Crosse, walked almost the whole way to Winona, got a ride to Red Wing, and called from there. His mother told him to sit tight, they would pick him up at the bus depot. Four years before, they had dropped him off at the same depot when he went off to boot camp.

Those first months home were like a Hemingway story. His mother had taught eighth grade all her life and for her education was a sacred thing, the more the better. Steve had the GI Bill, there was no money problem. He could go to Minneapolis and enroll in the University of Minnesota, or he could try Saint Olaf or Saint John's. Why, he could go anywhere he wanted!

"I'm going to Paris."

In the corner of the kitchen, the newspaper lowered and the old man looked briefly at him before once more raising his screen against the world. His mother's mouth was trying to make up its mind whether to smile or tremble.

"Paris," she repeated.

"Paris, France?" came from behind the newspaper.

"What school, Steve?" his mother asked, grasping at straws.

It was easier letting her think that once he got to France he would look into studying there, and as the days went by, she began to make arch allusions to the Grand Tour.

"Not all education takes place in the classroom, Stephen."

"That's what I've been saying."

She put her arms around him and hugged him tight. Declare victory and withdraw, that was the thing. She acted as if she had talked him into going.

He booked passage on a freighter leaving from New Orleans. They sailed on August 17. After more than a month of rolling passage on oily seas with scheduled and unscheduled calls he got off at Le Havre. In later years, his story of the six weeks he spent in France took shape from the telling; he himself half believed it had turned out all right. But the fact was he had a hell of a time even finding the station in Le Havre from which he took the train to Paris. The handicap of not knowing French was borne in upon him forcibly. He wandered Paris for two days before he had the courage to rent a room. His first effort, near the Boulevard Haussmann, left its mark. He had tried to rent a room in a brothel. He never forgot the derisive laughter that followed him into the street. Among the thoughts that came later was that James Jones would have chosen a girl and managed to move in with her. If Nicodemus had done that he might have learned French, and a few other things, and his life would have proceeded along very different lines than it did.

Returning from that benighted trip to France gave him far more the sense of homecoming than when he had come back from the marines a few months before. The one place he had felt at home in Paris was along the Seine, looking over the bookstalls that ran for blocks. Most of the titles were French, but there was the odd book in English. The only book he bought was a somewhat obscenely illustrated François Villon. Steve couldn't read the poems but as an artifact alone the book was desirable.

Once home, he went to Minneapolis, took the Fire Department test, was accepted, and spent the next twenty years on duty at a station off Franklin Avenue. The indolent life appealed to him, it gave him all the time in the world to read. The drills were more of a nuisance than actual fires. As soon as he was eligible for a pension, he retired.

Forty-one years old and retired. If he had stayed in the marines he could have retired at thirty-eight. He was by now totally immersed in books. Mabel, the librarian he had married, looked forward to going into the book business as much as Steve did. Their two daughters were students at the Minneapolis campus of the university. The mortgage on their house in South Minneapolis was paid up, the house itself was chock-full of books and the overflow was in the addition Steve had built to the garage. Those books were meant to be the base of the business they would now begin.

Buying the house a half mile east of Fairland in the southern part of the state was a calculated move. For one thing, it was a part of the state not crowded with book dealers, which from the point of view of acquisitions was important. As for sales, given the growing prominence of mail-order business, location was not as important as it had once been. Setting up in Minneapolis would have meant going against entrenched, multiple, and strong competition.

They bought the house, had the pool dug, put up the metal building behind the garage, and settled in. The girls graduated and married and were living in different states. Mabel still worked part-time in the Fairland Public Library and Steve spent his days either sitting at his desk in the store or attending auctions, garage sales, whatever, in search of books.

ZENO THE cat arched his back as the phone rang and Steve picked it up swiftly, if only to prevent another ring from disturbing the peace of the bookstore.

"Mr. Nicodemus? Stella Arthur."

"Yes."

"Does your offer still stand?"

"It does."

"Very well. I accept."

"Good."

"When can you come for them?"

The newly widowed Stella Arthur, like most people wanting to sell books, had been shocked to learn how little her late husband's library would bring. She had thought that at the least she could ask their original price and assumed that every book had increased in value.

"Do you realize how much money my husband spent on books?"

The Arthur house stood on a bluff overlooking the river. The library, a room twelve feet by twenty, high ceilinged with alcove shelving, contained perhaps four thousand volumes.

"Between seventy-five and a hundred thousand dollars."

Mrs. Arthur, in her forties, shapely, her ash blond hair cut short, seemed surprised at the figure. "Well, then."

"My offer is fifty cents a title. Some are worth more than that, others less."

She refused. Perhaps the one-hundred-thousand-dollar estimate had inflated her hopes. That had been two weeks ago. Nicodemus wondered if anyone else had even matched his offer. Transporting the books was no problem for him, which is why he had not figured it into his offer.

"I can come tomorrow, Mrs. Arthur."

"Fifty cents a title?"

"That's right."

"There are four thousand, one hundred and six books."

Nicodemus jotted down the number. "I'll bring a check."

Mabel came along to help him box the books. In her purse was a check for $2,053. With age and weight she looked shorter than she was, but she was a real help on a chore like this. They were partners all the way. If Steve had any regret it was that he had given Mabel full control of the accounts. Well, not exactly given her. She had always taken care of the household accounts, and when they were putting money away for the future, she had done the banking too. After they moved to Fairfield, it would have been too much of a hassle taking over the financial end as well. Mabel considered herself the better mathematician and she was probably right. All in all, it made sense that she kept the accounts and wrote the checks. Still it annoyed him. She had snorted when he suggested rounding the check off to $2,100.

"Why not to two thousand?"

"I don't want her to think I'm cheating her."

"You made an offer and she took it."

"Not right away."

"Of course not. No doubt she looked around to see if she could do better. It's pretty obvious she can't. I'm not giving her the check until we count the books either."

Her attitude might seem petty to him now, but during the years when he was a fireman Mabel's hard-headedness had made their dream possible. In the early years, her exact accounting kept them afloat. It was ridiculous to expect her to give up the habits of a lifetime now. And she was right. Mrs. Arthur wasn't doing them any favors.

The widow didn't object when she saw that Mabel was keeping a close account of the number of books as they got them into cartons. They were practiced at packing books, and had acquired a large supply of cardboard beer cases to facilitate the task. Mrs. Arthur lit a cigarette, leaned against a bookcase, and watched, monitoring the monitor. Two can play at this game.

Steve took some boxes into a far alcove where he lit his pipe. Before setting to work, he smoked meditatively for a time, thinking of the man who had built up this collection, for whom these books were the result of a lifetime quest. It seemed a little heartless of his widow to get rid of them so quickly. A few months ago, at the end of February, George Arthur had been the victim of a freak ice-fishing accident. It was not until spring that the body was found.

"Certainly not," Mrs. Arthur had said, when he asked if she was selling the house.

"These books represent years of collecting."

"Yes, they do. My husband was a devoted bibliophile. I am not. I think it would be as morbid of me to keep his books as to keep his clothing hanging in his closet. I am past my first grief, Mr. Nicodemus. I have been advised to be practical and that is what I intend to be."

Mabel had heard of the widow's reaction to the suggestion that she donate her husband's books to the Fairfield Library.

"What are those?" she had asked, pointing to some shelves of books just inside the main entrance.

"Those" were books the library was selling, books for which there was no longer sufficient call to warrant taking up shelf space.

"Most of my husband's books are older than those."

"But they wouldn't be just popular novels. That's what those are."

The librarian pleaded in vain. Standard library practice had given Mrs. Arthur the high ground. Her reaction had suggested that she meant to keep her husband's collection intact, but that theory was exploded when she contacted Nicodemus.

"I am surprised your husband never came to my store, Mrs. Arthur."

Her right brow arched slightly. "His favorite bookstores were in the Twin Cities, Cincinnati, and Chicago. Where are you located?"

Since she had found his telephone number, she knew the answer to that. Perhaps she had tried those Twin Cities stores to see if his offer was fair.

The room seemed to grow in size as the books disappeared from the shelves. The cases were stacked near the door. Steve would use a dolly to get them out to the van.

"I have three thousand, nine hundred and six," Mabel said when she was done. "You must have jumped a couple of hundred somewhere."

"You must have lost a couple of hundred somewhere," Mrs. Arthur shot back.

Steve was happy to leave the haggling to Mabel. Already he was looking forward to getting the books home and seeing what they had acquired. His preliminary sense that there were no enormously valuable books in the lot seemed borne out, but there were undeniably some very interesting items.

The two women reached a compromise and Mabel wrote a new check for $1,953. By that time, Steve had wheeled half the cartons out to the van. Their disagreement behind them, the two women stood in the now empty library.

"I intend to redecorate the whole house," Mrs. Arthur was saying. "But particularly this room. Of course those shelves will have to come out."

"I wish I'd bid on those," Steve said.

"Why don't you?"

"Let me know when you plan to have them removed."

She nodded.

In the van Mabel said, "They're very nice shelves but where would we put them?"

The shelving in the store was metal, durable, more practical than wood.

"Funny we never did business with him," Mabel said.

"What a way to go." He shivered.

Death by drowning was bad enough, but in a frozen lake! Poor Arthur's tragedy was their good luck. Steve was sure there would be some surprises among the books they had just bought, and the price, no matter Mabel's muttering, had been right.

TWO

STELLA WATCHED the van down the drive and into the street, a satisfied expression on her face. There went the books and the shelves were next. Soon the room would be restored to its original condition and look as it had when she was a girl. She wanted the house to be the Larson house again. Over the past seventeen years it had been increasingly referred to as the Arthur house, until Stella wondered if anyone at all remembered it as it had been when she lived there with her parents.

Her father had built the house, supervised its construction, wanting every square foot to express the pride he felt at being a success in this country. The Larson Lumberyard occupied acres between the railroad tracks and the river, accessible to two forms of transportation. From lumber her father's business branched out to include every sort of building material. He went into coal as well and eventually into fuel oil and gasoline, erecting a large service station on the corners of Apple and Jefferson. Harald Larson's forebears in Norway had been fishermen, but in this new country he became the leading entrepreneur in Fairland, Minnesota.

Stella Larson had been raised to think of herself as the daughter of the town's leading family and that is what she was. After attending the public grade school, she was sent away to the Visitation Convent in St. Paul, despite the Lutheran allegiance of her family.

Those four years were balanced, in a sense, by attendance at Gustavus Adolphus, from which she graduated at the age of twenty-two. She returned to Fairland in the hope and expectation that Roy Hunt would propose, and they would marry and live happily ever after in the place where they had both been children.

Two weeks after she came home that June her father died. He had been striding through the lumberyard when he stopped as if someone had tugged at his leash, looked around in a bewildered way, then crashed to the ground. He was dead before the ambulance arrived. Stella's mother, a fragile woman who had sat most of her life in a room with the shades half pulled, her workbasket on her lap, a cat asleep at her feet, sewing by the hour, was undone by her husband's death. But grief and loss were to be only a fraction of the shock awaiting Harald Larson's widow and daughter. The Larson empire, its emperor gone, began to totter. Bankers tried to explain to Stella's mother the nature of credit and how overextended Harald had been.

"His collateral was himself," Matthew Hunt said earnestly as if he were trying to explain something to himself. "With Harald gone..."

Things had to be sold off to pay the loans her father had outstanding at all three local banks and two in Minneapolis. Since her mother was incapable of grasping what was happening, it fell to Stella to preside over the dissolution of the Larson empire.

"If I were a man, this wouldn't be happening," she said to George Arthur when he bid for the lumberyard.

"If you had a husband, it wouldn't be happening."

He was in his mid-thirties, a relative newcomer to Fairland, handsome, Stella supposed, but so old, as he seemed to her. It turned out he was almost forty. But that wasn't the problem. He simply did not stir her heart in the way that Roy Hunt did. She was certain that if Roy were forty she would still feel the same way about him, but Roy was twenty-three and poor. Well, maybe not poor, but his future was all ahead of him. George Arthur, on the other hand, brought wealth with him to Fairland and he was using it to gobble up what her father had built over many years. When Stella dropped her head and glanced up at Arthur through her lashes it was the first move in a campaign to repossess her father's property.

"I love you, Stella," Roy Hunt said, perplexed that she was encouraging George Arthur.

"And I love you."

He tried to gather her to him, but she put both hands on his chest and held him off. They were sitting in her car, high above the river. Below them a barge full of coal moved slowly toward the Larson pier. Only it was no longer the Larson pier.

"Marry me, Stella."

"No. I am going to marry George Arthur."

"You don't love him."

"No, I love you. I told you that."

He fell back, looking as if he might cry. It was difficult not to contrast his helplessness with George Arthur's calm competence. "I don't understand you."

Stella took him in her arms and comforted him. She told him nothing would ever come between them, nothing important. Her marriage to George Arthur had nothing to do with them, nothing to do with love. It was a matter of simple business. George had the wherewithal to keep her father's acquisitions intact; Roy did not. If it had been necessary, she would have spelled out to Roy what she was suggesting, but when they moved into the backseat he stopped asking questions and the nature of their relationship was established. Furtive lovemaking with Roy would constitute the center of her emotional life. She would marry George Arthur as a way of preserving what her father had built over his lifetime.

"I am proposing marriage, Stella," George said to her a few nights after she had sealed her relation with Roy. They were dining in the sky room of the Belvedere Hotel, across from Fairland on the Wisconsin side of the river.

She put out her hand and let him take it in his.

"I will do everything to make you happy, Stella."

She exerted a slight pressure on his hand and smiled. She never made such promises to him. She would marry him but she would not pretend that he was the object of her passionate and consuming love. She did come to respect him, however, even though he was a daily reminder that she could not be the wife of Roy Hunt.

Roy never married. It would not have mattered if he had. Stella knew they were bound together in a far more primeval way, a way her wild ancestors along the fjords of her father's native land would understand. Roy went to work in his father's bank and like his father before him he made a modest profit off the adventuresome projects of others.

Stella never bore a child for George, thereby thwarting his ambition to leave a replica of himself upon the earth. That was a cold way of putting it; the desire to have children is not a theory, but she was determined that there would be no baby. And there was not. She lied shamelessly to George about unspecified female problems and took the pill religiously. She would have liked to have Roy's child, and from time to time the thought would occur that she might become pregnant by Roy and let George think the child was his. But if the deception worked he would *think* he had reproduced himself and she did not mean to provide him even that satisfaction.

Her thought that she was a part of the Larson empire he was acquiring was not her imagination. He said as much himself. Without her, to own what her father had built would have been incomplete. He had meant it as a compliment, perhaps, but she did not accept it as such. Not that they quarreled. They never quarreled. Their relationship was friendly. She did not hate him, at least she did not hate him when she forgot he was the usurper of her father's property and an obstacle to her marriage with Roy. He had many admirable qualities, she could see that. He had a good business head, he was kind to her, indeed tender and considerate when she lied to him about her inability to have children. But they drifted away from one another because of the lack of children, and his interest in books intensified.

When he redecorated what had been her father's billiard room, turning it into a library, Stella considered it a desecration. Among her fondest memories was playing billiards with her father in that room, but now it was all shelving and books and a desk in front of the great fireplace. She could not abide being in the library for longer than a few minutes. She never sat there. She hated George's books, irrationally, passionately.

"I could kill him," she said to Roy as she lay beside him in a motel halfway to Minneapolis.

Without his glasses, Roy had a bewildered look. He groped on the table beside the bed and found them. He lay back, naked under the sheet but wearing his glasses, staring at the ceiling.

"You'll outlive him. We both will."

"He is forty-seven years old and very healthy." She herself was thirty then. How old would she be when George died? If George died at the age her father had, she and Roy would be forty. Would Roy still want her then? Perhaps desire died. George's had. He became more and more obsessed with collecting books, poring over catalogues, going off on buying trips. She should have been glad he was so preoccupied but the sight of the library filled her with silent rage.

Roy's casual remark that she would outlive George seemed somehow a promise and as the years passed Stella became impatient. When Roy came to the house to talk banking business with George, the difference in their ages was palpable to Stella. Roy was of a different generation. And so was she. Stella left the two men alone on such occasions. Eventually she would be made privy to the conversation, informed by each of them separately.

George's passion was to keep as much money out of the tax collector's hands as possible. His investments aimed at this, hardly an unusual thing, but there was more.

"He has a great deal of cash around the house," Stella told Roy.

"How do you mean?"

"He hides money at home."

"How much?"

She counted it at Roy's urging. In the box on the shelf of his closet there was forty-seven thousand dollars in cash. Roy was appalled.

"It could be earning interest."

"Perhaps. And it could also be taxed."

George did business in cash when he could and this was particularly the case when he bought and sold books.

"But the books are an asset," Roy objected.

"Not a taxable one."

The thought of that much money sitting around plagued the banker in Roy Hunt. Chiefly the thought of its not earning interest, but also its vulnerability. It could be stolen. If there was a fire, it could be destroyed. Thinking of such possibilities made Roy look bewildered even with his glasses on. Stella agreed to discuss the matter with George.

"What is all that money doing in your closet?" she asked her husband.

He was sitting in the library reading, and he looked up at her over his half glasses.

"It is ours."

"I didn't think it wasn't. But why do you keep it here?"

He put down his book and removed his glasses. It was the longest she had ever been in the library, listening to him explain. Her heart went out to him as he spoke and she had to actively resist comparing him with her father. George had come out of poverty into riches, by luck and cunning and persistence. But he knew that it might not have happened and, having happened, could be rapidly undone.

"Wealth is a fragile thing, Stella, as I needn't tell you. One day your father was the wealthiest man in town. He died and the vultures moved in on him. I mean the bankers. He should have taken that into account."

"He didn't plan to have a stroke."

The cash in the house was George's hedge against disaster. But what of theft and fire? He frowned.

"These books are here and some are very valuable."

"But books can be insured."

"Insured, yes, but not replaced, not all of them."

"But money, George. Cash! That's different."

"Not all of it is in the house."

"But what if something should happen to us?"

Once the topic had been opened, Stella returned to it again and again.

"Put it into a safe-deposit box at the bank, George. It makes me nervous to have so much money around the house."

He shook his head. "Then it would become the prey of the IRS."

"I'll bet Roy could figure out a way."

He had already told her he could. Not precisely in keeping with the ethical code of banking, but Roy could provide George Arthur with the Fairland equivalent of an anonymous Swiss account. Assign him a safe-deposit box without recording it. The bank would keep one key, George the other, in the usual way, but there would be no record at the bank that the box belonged to George Arthur.

George did not like the idea. "The whole point of that money is that no one knows we have it."

"But no one would know."

"The bank would know."

"Only Roy would know."

The fact was that George trusted Roy, and had every reason to do so. But it took nearly two years before he agreed to put the money in a safe-deposit box. Even before Stella and Roy knew the full amount—seven hundred and fifty thousand dollars—the plan had formed in their mind.

In a Minneapolis hotel, they entered an elevator on the floor where their room was, and confronted Dr. Poeglin and his wife. Before the elevator reached the lobby, it had obviously dawned on Babs Poeglin that there was something odd about meeting Stella Arthur and Roy Hunt together in a Minneapolis hotel. Perhaps their original reaction when they met the doctor and his wife stirred suspicion, but Stella had the definite feeling that the Poeglins did not believe her when she left Roy and them in the lobby with the excuse that she must meet George.

On the drive back to Fairland, Roy kept saying that the Poeglins hadn't suspected a thing, but he was clearly whistling in the dark. What would George do if he learned she had been unfaithful to him? Not just once but for years? He would divorce her. She knew that without the shadow of a doubt. When George Arthur owned something he wanted exclusive possession. The thought that another man had made love to his wife would be intolerable to him.

That the man she regarded as the unjust possessor of her father's wealth might put *her* away angered Stella. Nor was she placated when Roy assured her there would be an equal division of the property. The prospect that Stella might be free to marry, even at the price of scandal, noticeably cheered Roy. But the prospect could not please Stella if it meant relinquishing her father's house to George.

"I wish he would die," she said with sudden vehemence.

"I wouldn't count on it. George looks pretty healthy to me."

"My father looked healthy too."

She realized that at some time in the dark unconscious depths of her soul she had decided that George Arthur would not outlive her father. That is, he would not live to a more advanced age than Harald Larson. Her father had died at fifty-six. George was now fifty-five.

When George agreed to transfer the cash from the house to an unregistered safe-deposit box in Roy's bank, Stella had the sense that they were sequestering it from her husband. She wanted that cash, but she wanted everything else as well. As George's only heir, she would get it all when he died. Both she and George received a copy of the key to the box and Stella put the thin little red envelope containing hers among her jewelry.

Perhaps every wife has imagined her husband dead and herself a widow. From an actuarial point of view, it was bound to happen eventually. Stella could not wait for eventually. She felt she had already given too many of the best years of her life to a man she did not love. In the weeks after she and Roy had run into the Poeglins in the hotel elevator in Minneapolis, Stella began consciously to plot her husband's death.

"Kill him?" Roy asked, a funny little smile playing on his lips.

"I don't want him finding out about us, not now."

"He won't."

"We know the Poeglins saw us. What if others did and we don't know it? George would kill you if he found out."

An inspired remark, however dubious it might be. Once Roy imagined his own life under threat from a jealous George, he entered less reluctantly into the discussion as to how George would die.

One afternoon in the Hunt cabin on the shore of Lake Owatonna, Stella, their lovemaking done, had gone into the kitchen to make coffee when she looked out at the lake and was surprised to see cars parked on its frozen surface.

"They're ice fishing," Roy explained.

"But aren't the cars too heavy?"

"Sometimes in the spring a quick thaw will surprise a fisherman. Cars have sunk that way."

"What are those little shacks?"

"They sit in them while they fish. It protects them from the wind. Some bring heaters with them."

It was the fact that they made a hole in the ice through which to drop their line that suggested the idea. She could tell from Roy's reaction that it could be done. Two evenings later, at the house, Roy invited George ice fishing on Lake Owatonna.

"Ice fishing!" George made a face. "Roy, I don't fish in the summer."

"This is a wholly different experience."

"And one I am willing to forgo."

"What's it like?" Stella asked Roy. The idea was too good to permit George to dismiss it like this.

An extended discussion of ice fishing followed and George reluctantly entered into it.

"I think you've made a convert of Stella," he said to Roy. "You should take her."

"I'm certainly not going without you. George, let's try it. We've never done anything at all like it. It could be fun."

How ironic that in the end he agreed to go as a favor to her.

The night before, Roy widened the ice hole in the shack they would use. The plan was simple. The door of the shack would be opened, George would be pushed inside, he would disappear through the ice, and Roy would make sure he never came up again. Simple. Except that a dozen things could happen that would defeat their purpose.

A membrane of new ice could form over the hole and save George's life.

"I'll go out first and make sure it's still open," Roy said.

There could be other fishermen nearby who would see or hear something that would make their claim of an incredible accident suspicious.

But they would go on a weekday, and if there were many fishers on the ice, they would not go through with it.

They enumerated every conceivable eventuality. The one thing they did not foresee was a blizzard.

On the appointed day, Stella woke to frosted windows and the roar of the wind around the house. She cleared a pane to look out, and saw the trees bowing in the fierce wind and snow flying thick and relentless. Her heart sank. Today would not be the day.

Nonetheless, Roy came to the door as planned at seven-thirty. Stella and George, still in pajamas, were dawdling over breakfast when he arrived. Roy was astounded they were not ready.

"The snow? That makes it perfect. The fish will bite with a vengeance in weather like this."

George was not sportsman enough to see the implausibility of this. He rose from the table. If anything, he seemed glad to get the silly excursion out of the way. Roy gave Stella a significant look and she went to get ready.

After they left the highway, Roy drove up an unplowed and slippery road toward the lake.

"If we get stuck in here, we'll never get out," George groaned.

He sat next to Roy in the front seat. Behind them, Stella realized that George would not be coming back this road ever again. It seemed a thought like any other.

At the cabin, Roy donned snowshoes and said he would check the shack. While he plodded toward the lake, George made a fire.

"We'll want this when we come back."

"Yes."

From the window, Stella watched as Roy reached the fishing shack on the frozen lake and opened the door. He stepped inside and seemed to have been erased from the landscape. The thought that something might happen to him out there, that he might accidentally slip through the ice, filled her with sudden panic. She turned to where George was still busy with the fire.

"Let's go," she said.

"Wasn't Roy coming back for us?"

"And then walk all the way back to the shack?"

"That doesn't make much sense, does it? I hate to leave this fire."

"It'll be safe. Put the fire screen in front of it."

"I wasn't worried about the cabin. I hate to leave the warmth."

Stella was already putting on her heavy jacket. She was still wearing her boots. She wanted to shout at George and tell him to hurry, get dressed, let's go. He slowly withdrew from the fire and then as the relative coldness of the rest of the room made itself felt, pulled on his jacket.

"I don't know why I ever agreed to this, Stella."

"It could be fun."

Whatever she said now would seem awful. It was better when they were outside and the wind off the lake snatched words from their mouths before they could be heard. George was shouting something. Stella made a visor of her gloved hand and peered out at the lake. Roy stood beside the shack, waving them to come on.

Stella went first, trying to use the footprints Roy had made earlier, but his stride was too much for her shorter legs and she made slow progress. From time to time she turned to see George trudging after her, chin on his chest, following her tracks. It was important not to think that she was leading him to his death.

It was over so quickly she could hardly believe it. When she reached the shack, Roy did not look at her but stared intently at the approaching George. As soon as he drew up to the shack, Roy opened the door with one hand and with the other pushed George inside. He closed the door after him and stood with his back pressed against it, his terrified eyes fixed on Stella. The only sound was the keening sound of the wind, driving the snow before it. Stella pressed her ear against the side of the shack. She could hear nothing from within.

She gestured to Roy to look inside. She herself stood back as Roy pulled the door open. George's head and arms were visible. He was trying to extricate himself from the freezing water, but he could get no purchase on the slippery surface. His eyes lifted wildly to Roy and went past him to Stella. The pleading look died and was replaced by comprehension. Then Roy put a boot on his shoulder and pushed: he slipped beneath the surface, his accusing eyes burning into her.

THREE

ONCE WHEN he was nine years old, playing on the bluffs overlooking the river, Roy slipped, lost his footing, and clung to the ledge for what seemed hours before the boys he was with managed to pull him back up onto the narrow path. Once on the path again he lay face down, pressing himself from head to toe as flat against the solid surface as he could. When he finally got the courage to stand he faced the wall of the cliff, not daring to look down at the rocks and river over which he had precariously hung. He never went on such a hike again. For years afterward he had had an awful dream in which his fingers slipped and lost their hold and he plummeted down, lazily, endlessly, but always waking in a sweat before he hit bottom. He would sit up in bed and stare into the dark wondering if he had cried out or if that too was part of the dream.

Watching George Arthur slip out of sight beneath the water was like watching himself complete the fall begun so many years ago when he was nine.

He went inside the shack and sat on the stool and waited, staring at the dark ring of water, wondering if George would rise again. He didn't. As time went by it was possible to think that it had not happened. Stella crowded in and stood beside him. There was nothing comforting in her presence, nothing desirable in the bulky pressure she exerted against him. They waited half an hour and then trudged slowly back to the cabin.

It took an hour and a half for the fire truck and ambulance and a deputy sheriff to arrive. Stella stayed by the fire in the cabin while Roy led the volunteer firemen and deputy sheriff out across the lake. The wind was even more violent now, and everything was done in silence and with gestures. People shouted even when they did not expect to be heard, counting on their waving arms to convey their meaning. At the shack, Roy opened the door and pointed.

The man who had driven the fire truck went inside and Roy followed him. The echoed sound of the wind seemed to rise an octave.

"No wonder," the man said. "That's the size of a manhole."

"It was his first time."

The hatchet with which Roy had enlarged the hole and chipped away the coat of ice that had formed during the night still lay inside the shack. The fireman picked it up and looked at it.

"Did you see him go through?" he asked Roy.

"No."

"You didn't see him? Then how do you know he fell through?"

"What else could have happened? I was fishing in there." He pointed at a shack twenty yards off. "I came to see how he was doing and the shack was empty. I figured he must have headed in without telling me. So I went back to the cabin. He wasn't there. His wife hadn't seen him. That's when I called you."

The fireman didn't like it. He liked even less the prospect of sending a man into the water. But the body suits and snorkels had been carried out onto the ice.

"Is his car still here?"

Roy looked blank and bewildered. On the one hand, he wanted this over with. On the other, there were advantages to encouraging the fireman's skepticism. The more time that elapsed the less doubt that George was really and truly out of the picture at last.

They trudged back to the cabin. The three of them had come in Roy's car and it was where he had parked it. Could he have walked anywhere?

"Where would he walk in weather like this?"

Stella turned a stunned, numb look at the professional rescuers.

"You didn't see him?"

The fireman cast the question at Stella like a hopeless fisherman. He did not wait for her answer, but turned and began to shout orders. They would proceed as if there was no doubt that a man had slipped through the ice and drowned. Unspoken in his orders was the assumption that if they found the body at all they would not find it alive.

They did not find the body.

Two divers took turns going down and each of them slid beneath the frigid water half a dozen times before darkness descended. Back in the cabin, the fireman looked at Stella as if he expected her to rail at him.

"The currents out there could have done anything."

That was when Stella's eyes filled with tears. Roy felt like crying himself. But it was himself, not George, he felt sorry for. Now he had the burden of guilt to carry for the rest of his life. He had killed George Arthur and he would never be able to forget it.

The fire truck and ambulance drove away, followed by the deputy sheriff. Roy and Stella stayed in the cabin. Alone, they had little to say to one another. The thought of taking her in his arms filled Roy with a strange dread. Stella had been the driving force in this, his Lady Macbeth.

Would either of them have been able to face it if they had known then that it would be three months before George's body was found? Roy knew he would not have been. Alone with Stella, the room illumined only by the dying flicker of the fire George had lit, Roy stood at the picture window and looked out at the scarcely visible lake. The surface was covered by swirls and arabesques of snow bordering mirrorlike spots of ice; the ice shacks faded into the horizon. Stella came and stood next to him but some instinct prevented them from touching one another. He did not have to ask to know that she was thinking the same thing he was. Out there, in the dark, under the ice, in frigid water, the drowned body of George Arthur drifted with the water of the lake. Why did he fear that somehow George would rise up from his watery grave, ascend through the ice, and point the finger of accusation at his murderers?

"Let's go back to town and wait," Stella said softly.

He hesitated, as if leaving the scene, leaving George to be discovered by someone else, jeopardized them. He did not voice these irrational thoughts and they went back to town to wait.

To wait! They thought it would be only a matter of hours. That it might be days would have seemed impossible then. But that he would have returned to work before George's body was discovered, that he and Stella would have to enter into an extended charade, avoiding one another, not doing anything that would arouse curiosity, was a prospect Roy never dreamed of.

"You two go ice fishing often?" Oscar Ewbank, the sheriff, asked, his little pig eyes sliding around Roy's office.

"Never before. It was George's first time."

"You took him out in that kind of weather?"

Roy waited, shook his head slowly from side to side as if in mild rebuke. "I couldn't get him to put it off. We had agreed to go out on Tuesday and Tuesday it had to be."

"That was a regular blizzard, Roy."

"You're telling me? I was out on that goddamn lake in it."

"Tell me about that."

"What do you think I'm doing?"

"I mean the details. You were in different shacks?"

"Oscar, you ever been ice fishing?"

"Not lately."

"The size of those shacks is no bigger than it's ever been."

"So you were fishing in different shacks."

"I put him in one. Showed him how to keep the hole open."

"He had a hatchet with him."

"In the shack, yes. He needed it to chop away ice if it formed."

"He chopped it away all right. Did you see the size of that hole?"

"How do you mean?"

"There couldn't have been much more than open water in that shack when he got done using that hatchet."

Roy said nothing.

"You know there are people who still think he didn't drown at all."

"I hope to God they're right." The fervor with which he said it visibly impressed Oscar. It was not feigned. Roy had reached the point where he would have given anything to live over the events of that Tuesday afternoon.

"Did the sheriff come see you?" Stella asked when she phoned him that night.

"They haven't found any trace of him yet."

"Maybe he did just walk away and we didn't notice."

Roy did not answer. To have Stella say that seemed to cheat him of the credit for doing the awful thing he had done. Did she think someone might hear her speaking to him? It would have been paranoid to imagine her phone was tapped. Phone tapping in Fairland! That was crazy.

"You mustn't give up hope," he said finally, playing the game.

They could not see one another and the phone calls were worse than dissatisfying. All the years they had risked discovery haunted his memory. That hotel elevator in Minneapolis and the curious stares of the Poeglins had been the turning point. Because of that they had arranged the ice-fishing accident. Two weeks after George Arthur was reported missing—that is the most Oscar said he would admit to—Louis Poeglin came into Roy's office.

"I want to expand the clinic," he said breezily. "I've already engaged an architect. You got any money you want to loan?"

Throughout the ensuing discussion, through the negotiations that continued afterward, Roy tried unsuccessfully to shake the idea that Poeglin was blackmailing him. It was a totally irrational idea. He knew that. He explained that to himself. It didn't help. Nor did it help to admit that Poeglin's figures and projections amply supported the judgment that he should expand. A banker would have to be an idiot not to back a medical man in circumstances like these. Nor did Poeglin expect anything other than the standard interest on a half-million-dollar loan over ten years. Against all the evidence and his better judgment, Roy Hunt sat across from Poeglin and thought the doctor understood perfectly well what had happened to Stella's husband and was there to be bought off.

Early in March there was a week of unseasonably warm weather. Passing cars sent sprays of slushy water at dodging pedestrians. The sun glistened. The sparrows that stayed the winter nonetheless looked like harbingers of spring as they flitted from branch to leafless branch. The river ran swiftly, spangled with the sun. At noon, skipping lunch, Roy drove to the cabin. Stella's car was parked behind it, her rear bumper flush against the slanted door of the storm cellar.

At the sound of the cabin door opening, she turned, her face contorted with terror.

"Oh my God, you scared me."

"Who else would know where the key is?"

"It's the first place anyone would look."

"If anyone sees us they'll think we arranged to meet."

He did not touch her. He had not touched her since that Tuesday, and desire was so remote as to be unimaginable. He went past her into the front room and looked out at the lake. Still solidly frozen. Were there fewer ice shacks than before? The ones that remained looked abandoned. No one would fish that lake while there was the chance a drowned body might catch on their hook. If he expected her to join him at the window he was mistaken. When he returned to the kitchen she sat at the trestle table, her car coat open, legs crossed, holding a cup of coffee in both hands.

"This is instant. The water's hot if you want any."

He made a cup and sat across from her. The sun coming through the window lay on her ash blond hair. Her lips, plush and red, formed a slight smile.

"This isn't what we bargained for, is it, Roy?"

"Some day the ice will thaw."

"In the spring."

He could have struck the table with frustration. Spring was weeks away. Nor with the thaw was there any guarantee that Oscar Ewbank would resume the search for the body. The police in Des Moines had telexed a probable sighting of George Arthur and the sheriff had gone down to check.

Roy said, "When he's found, his will goes into effect."

"So?"

"I think you should get the money out of that deposit box. I'd feel a lot better if I didn't have that unaccounted-for box."

"You'd feel better?"

"Because it would be safer."

"For you. What about me, with that kind of money sitting around the house? Remember the arguments you used with George."

Her tone was almost accusing, as if what had happened to George had been Roy's idea alone.

"We can hide it."

"George hid it."

It was a conversation they were destined to have again and again. He told her if the money were found, the IRS would be down on her like a chicken hawk, audit George's books, and check them against his returns. The feds would love to grab that money for unpaid taxes.

"I thought the money was anonymous and safe in the bank."

"I mean if something goes wrong."

"What could go wrong?"

"Stella, any day of the week one of the employees could come upon that box and wonder what the explanation is."

"How would they open it?"

"They can't *open* it. But why is it locked if it isn't assigned?"

"You clean it out as soon as that happens."

He recognized the remark as one he had made to George Arthur.

"Let's clean it out now."

She shook her head. "I am not going down to the bank and rummage around in safe-deposit boxes while the search for my missing husband continues."

She might have been taunting him.

IN APRIL, within one week, the snow disappeared except for a few gray ridges along the road leading to the cabin. The lake was free of ice now. Roy parked behind the cabin and went down to the boat-house. The lock was stiff from disuse, as if it too had to thaw. Inside the low building, Roy lowered his fishing boat into the water, got the outboard mounted, and pushed off, hopping in at the same time. The boat glided through the opened doors of the boat-house onto the lake. He let it drift out a way before starting the motor. The racket of the outboard seemed to reverberate from the shore behind him and to move in concentric circles of sound out onto the lake.

To head for the spot where the fishing shacks had stood was silly, but then it was silly for him to go out alone looking for the drowned body of George Arthur. The body would rise of its own accord now and was as likely to be found washed ashore as anywhere. The thought made Roy want to gag. His only protection was the unreal character the events of last winter had taken on with the passage of months.

He reached the approximate location of the fishing shacks and then made a great leisurely turn. His intention had been to head for the eastern shore and work his way slowly around the lake, keeping an eye out for George, but when he got the little boat about he saw the figure standing on his dock.

Oscar Ewbank.

Roy conquered the impulse to head for the far shore and flee. He aimed the prow directly at the dock and revved the motor up to full speed. Behind him a large chevron formed as he moved toward the sheriff. He circled and came alongside.

"Get in, Oscar."

The sheriff squinted, causing his little eyes to disappear entirely.

"What are you doing?"

"Same thing you are, I suspect."

Oscar didn't answer that. But he didn't get into the boat.

"They're bringing the launch and we'll go out in that, Roy."

"Use the public access, won't you?" A chicken point, but Roy did not want Oscar's men pulling a trailer with a launch on it across his property.

"See anything out there?"

"I wasn't out ten minutes, Oscar."

"We'll take it from here."

"He should be coming to the surface."

"Let's hope so. This must be difficult for Mrs. Arthur."

"Have you talked with her lately?"

"Haven't you?"

Roy hung his head. "It's hard. I feel half responsible for George's death."

"If we don't find him, he ain't dead."

"I don't think she'll take much comfort from that, Oscar."

"You may be right."

They did not find George's body the first day, or the second. But when they went out on the fourth day—they skipped Sunday—the body was spotted in a cove on the western shore. Over the past three months it had drifted four hundred yards. Oscar asked Roy to identify the body.

"You all knew him."

"Just a formality."

The rubbery bag was laid on Roy's dock and he went reluctantly down to it. One of Oscar's assistants unzipped the bag and pulled down the flap. Despite the water and cold and passage of time, there was no doubt that the puckered, marble-white, lightly bearded face was that of George Arthur. Later, Roy thought it was the sight of that posthumous beard that did it. In any case, he hung over the lake and vomited violently.

As if they were ashamed of his reaction, Oscar and his men zipped up the bag and set off toward the cabin where the widow stood on the front deck, her hands held slightly from her body, as if she had stopped in the act of raising or lowering them from her eyes.

The Fairland *Courier,* which had been running ambiguous stories on the disappearance of a leading citizen, now decided that George Arthur deserved the biggest civic send-off the town could provide. Roy found the ceremony in the auditorium of the high school redundant. It was difficult to act as if he were simply adjusting to the thought of George as really dead when the memory of the man disappearing under the ice months ago was still vivid to him. The mayor, a party hack named Hennings, went on and on about the elements of the Arthur business enterprises and Roy could see that Stella was gritting her teeth. Hennings might have been calling the inventory of her father's achievements and attributing them to her departed husband. Roy had refused a seat on the stage and sat in the front row from which he had all too good a view of the small burnished bronze urn that sufficed to hold the cremated remains of George Arthur.

Stella had agreed that in the coming week, as she looked after the grim business of being a new widow, they would open the secret safe-deposit box.

FOUR

MRS. ARTHUR called to ask Nicodemus if he wanted the shelves on which her husband's library had reposed, but he declined to bid. He still had not unpacked the books and the call did not prod him to do so. The gruesome story of how George Arthur had spent the winter beneath the frozen surface of Lake Owatonna seemed to affect the very cartons containing the man's books. Besides, with the advent of spring, Nicodemus spent the days he did not open the store sitting in the sun beside the still empty pool, reading Dickens. He was in the process of reading through all of Dickens again.

It was a comforting thought that he would never run out of books to read, even if he confined himself to rereading the tried and true. One could always return to Dickens and Trollope and Thackeray, to James and Howells and Twain.

"And Jane Austen," Mabel added primly.

"Ca va sans dire," Nicodemus said with a smile.

Mabel's part-time job in the Fairland Public Library had brought a new dimension to her interest in books. In Minneapolis her reading had been literature; in Fairland she had acquired a taste for trash, trash meaning Edgar Rice Burroughs, Zane Grey, Stephen King, Louis L'Amour, writers who produced books at an incredible clip, commanded a wide readership, and whose reputations would go the way of F. Marion Crawford's and the other Winston Churchill's, authors well represented on the shelves of the Nicodemus Bookstore. Mabel listened to the call from Mrs. Arthur and came out to the store minutes after he hung up.

"Why not buy the shelves?"

"We don't need them."

"I've been thinking." She held the elbow of one arm and put a hand under her chin. "Those shelves would set off the rare books very nicely."

"Mabel, anyone who knows the value of a book does not need an impressive setting for it."

"I think you're wrong."

It was clear she wished to argue the point and clearer that she would persist until they made a bid on the Arthur bookshelves. In quest of peace and quiet, he agreed to go.

"When?"

He had been about to retire to the yard with *The Old Curiosity Shop*. "I suppose I could go up there now."

"Better phone to say you're coming."

"No need for that. I'll go right now."

He took the Dickens with him. His thought was to go to the coffee shop in the Viking Motel and read there for an hour or so and then go home and tell Mabel the shelves had already been sold. But the way she had brought up the subject made that a risky course. He decided he would first drive to the house and hope Mrs. Arthur's asking price was sufficiently unrealistic that he could just turn it down and go.

Driving the van up the sweeping driveway again, Nicodemus felt like a tradesman, but Mrs. Arthur had not objected to his coming to the main entrance under the porte cochere before. Today there was a low pearl-gray sports car parked there. Nicodemus pulled up behind it, keeping a prudent distance. The little car looked so fragile he feared a tap from the bumper of the van would do irreparable damage—or worse, all too reparable damage for which he would have to pay.

The day was warm and Nicodemus wore only a corduroy jacket over his plaid shirt. Under cover of the porte cochere, out of the reach of the sun, he shivered. Pressing the bell, he felt uncomfortable, as if he had never been there before.

The woman who came to the door was not Mrs. Arthur. Perhaps thirty, thick reddish hair pulled back tightly on her head, she smiled out at him as if she could not see him.

"Yes?"

"Mrs. Arthur called me about the bookshelves."

The pretty little nose wrinkled.

"When did she call?"

He pushed back his sleeve. "Half an hour ago?"

"She must have called you from downtown."

"My name is Nicodemus. I bought the books and she wondered if I wanted to bid on the shelves."

The door was pushed open. "Come on in. I'm Mrs. Arthur's niece, Rosemary Burnet."

Rosemary did interior decorating and she was there to study the house and develop some concepts. She came into the library with Nicodemus and stood in the doorway shaking her head.

"The things I could do with this room after those shelves are gone."

"Like what?"

"It doesn't matter. This room is to look exactly as it did when my aunt was a girl. It was her father's billiard room and that is what she wants it to be again. By and large I have carte blanche in the other rooms. Those are very good shelves."

"Too good for me, I'm afraid. Any bid I'd be willing to make she would rightly take as an insult. I don't really need them."

"You already have shelves for the books?"

He nodded.

"How many books do you have?"

"I'm a dealer."

They were fellow tradesmen now. She said, "I wouldn't mind having those shelves myself. If I owned them I know I'd think of ways to use them, maybe all at once, maybe in a number of jobs."

"How much would you give for them?"

She laughed a musical laugh. "I would remind her I am her niece and ask for a deal."

"Maybe we could make a joint bid?"

"Want a Diet Pepsi? I'm having one."

It wasn't a cup of coffee but it would do. Rosemary reminded him a bit of his daughter Thea. He followed her into the kitchen where she pulled open the fridge, leaned back for a moment, and then swooped for two cans. She handed him one.

"We're not stealing. I brought these."

Rosemary had just driven down from Minneapolis where her business was located. They returned with their soft drinks to the library, which echoed in its emptiness.

"Maybe this will all be mine someday," Rosemary said, assuming a theatrical expression and sweeping her arm around.

"You're her niece?"

"Once removed, as they say. We've always kept in touch but what happened to her husband has brought us closer together."

"Hmmm."

"You know what happened to her husband, don't you?"

"He drowned."

She tipped her head to one side. "That's like saying we dropped an explosive device on Hiroshima. He wasn't found for months. Can you imagine what that was like for her? Anyway, I got into the habit of coming down and staying with her weekends. Just so she wouldn't feel completely alone."

"Is she alone?"

"They had no children."

He had the impression that she was talking to him for the same reason he was listening to her, and indeed the conversation soon turned to the bookstore. She was surprised to be told that Fairland was a good location.

"Even better than I thought when we moved here."

"Moved from where?"

"Minneapolis."

"Minneapolis! Where in Minneapolis?"

He let her believe that he had been in the book business in Minneapolis too, which wasn't entirely false, but he did not want to tell her he had been a fireman. She was clearly impressed by what he did now and mentioning those twenty years spent acquiring the pension that had made becoming a bookseller possible would have taken some of the romance out of his profession. She was interested in hearing about the buying and selling of used books and he was happy to oblige.

"I'd like to see your store."

"We're open three days a week."

"Three days a week," she repeated with a little smile. "It must be tough."

"It gives me time to go look at bookshelves I don't really want."

She went over to the nearest alcove and peered at the shelves. Finally she took glasses from her bag and put them on.

"I don't know why I pretend I can see without these."

Nicodemus pushed his bifocals higher on his nose. The fact that he had them on seemed a disavowal of vanity.

She said, "These are unbelievably well made."

"It's foolish to get rid of them. They were made for this room."

"But she sold the books." She turned to face him. "Which was already kind of dumb, wasn't it? I wouldn't have minded having them."

"Come buy them back."

"How much?"

"Five thousand dollars."

"Ouch. That's too rich for me. Believe me, it couldn't have been the money with Aunt Stella. She doesn't need five thousand dollars."

"Oh, I gave her less than half that."

"And you want to charge me five!"

"If I sold at the price I bought I wouldn't be in business long, would I?"

She laughed, then grew serious. "When I first saw this room empty I could have cried. It's not that I knew it well, but I have memories of George here. He spent most of his leisure time with his books. I'd give anything if Stella would buy the books back and fill up these shelves again.''

"It can't be a library and a billiard room at the same time."

"She could have had a billiard table in the basement. Or upstairs. But that wouldn't do. She wants her father's billiard room again."

They were still talking when Mrs. Arthur came home. She was surprised to see Nicodemus.

"I had second thoughts about the shelves."

"Do you want them?"

"Now I've had third thoughts. I guess not."

"What's wrong with them?"

"As I said to Rosemary, they belong in this room. Take them out of here and they drop in value enormously."

"Take them."

"Mrs. Arthur, I can't afford..."

"I mean just take them. I want them gone."

"You mean you'd *give* them away?"

"Stella!" Rosemary cried. "You're not serious."

Her niece's shock seemed to snap her out of it. How the value of the shelves plummeted with her suggestion that he simply take them away.

"You act as if you want them, Rosemary."

"I do. I've decided. I'll take them. I'll put them in a warehouse and use them eventually. But I won't let you just throw them out."

"Throw them out? I offered them to Mr. Nicodemus."

If it hadn't been for the delight of meeting Rosemary, Nicodemus would have wished he had gone to the Viking Coffeehouse instead.

"I wish you'd given me the books too," Rosemary said.

"Where would you put that many books?"

Rosemary cocked her head at Nicodemus, then said to her aunt, "Did you go through all the books?"

"We got an exact count, didn't we, Mr. Nicodemus."

But Rosemary said, "I meant did you check them, see what he might have hidden in them."

"Hidden!"

"Once when I was here he got up and took a book off the shelf. He wanted to give me some money. He had it in the book."

"How much money?"

"They were fifty-dollar bills."

After a moment, Mrs. Arthur said that she doubted her husband had filled all his books with fifty-dollar bills.

"We should keep them in the family anyway."

"I didn't think. And now it's too late." She turned to Nicodemus. "Isn't it?"

"They're for sale."

"As a single lot?"

"Stella, I can't afford it," Rosemary said.

"I can afford it."

"Five thousand dollars?"

Mrs. Arthur turned slowly to face Nicodemus. "How much?"

Again he explained that he could not sell for the same price at which he had bought.

"Now I'm glad you didn't accept the shelves."

Rosemary came to the door with him. "I really would like to see your store."

He gave her a card. When he eased the van around the sport car, Nicodemus wished he drove something less practical.

HE TOLD Mabel that Mrs. Arthur had given the bookshelves to her niece who was an interior decorator and that ended that. He went into the bookstore, locking the door after him since it wasn't a business day, and settled himself at his desk with several of the boxes of George Arthur's books on the floor around him. They had boxed the books following the order of the shelves and Arthur had his books arranged according to categories of his own devising. Nicodemus decided to look first at the man's specialty, the Spanish conquest of America, since there was far more chance of finding something valuable there.

The eighteenth-century volumes published in Madrid might prove valuable. He set them beside his desk in preparation for checking some catalogues later. The next book was a paperback published in Salamanca only a few years before, the history of the influence of the University of Salamanca on the universities founded in the New World. He was about to put it back in the box when he decided to flip through it. His Spanish was serviceable and there seemed to be a lot of photographs. The small red envelope fell on the floor when he fanned the book open.

FIVE

THE LADIES Benevolent Society of the Unitarian church was devoted to good works in the community and abroad. They took charge of the parish soup kitchen three times a month, collected donations for various Central American causes, agitated for more effective sex education in our schools—and played duplicate bridge all Thursday afternoon in the parish hall.

A soup kitchen in Fairland was more an idea than an activity, sending money to leftist governments was effectively handled by Claudia Cartwright the pastor, and concern for sex education was another of Claudia's hobbyhorses, but the bridge was a serious matter. Babs Poeglin had not missed an afternoon of duplicate for seven years, beginning when Chester Harkness had been their pastor, his term coming to an inglorious end because of the unfortunate arrest in the men's room of the bus depot. Not that the parishioners abandoned him. Chet just felt it was time to get out of Fairland. So Claudia was hired. Her interests had their effect on the Benevolent Society, but duplicate bridge remained for some of its members the cement that held the parish together. In the secret fastness of her heart Babs Poeglin equated Thursday afternoon bridge with her Unitarian faith.

There are women for whom bridge is an excuse to get out of the house, a chance to gossip, to have an extra glass of wine, but duplicate permits none of these. Which, until the episode in the hotel elevator in Minneapolis, was perfectly all right with Babs. A little chat before and after bridge more than sufficed for her. But the expression on the faces of Stella Arthur and Roy Hunt when that elevator door slid open like a stage curtain was something she could not drive from her mind.

Louis in his infuriating way had resolutely refused to find anything suspicious about their being in Minneapolis together.

"She said she was going to meet George," he stated flatly, gazing ahead at the featureless expanse of the Interstate taking them south to Fairland. Louis was three monkeys in one, refusing to see, hear, or speak evil.

"Then why did they look so guilty?"

"Is that how they looked?"

"Honestly. Did you even see them?"

Basically, Louis was a prude. If he did believe that Stella and Roy were misbehaving, he would feel obliged to sever all social relations with them, although he would no doubt continue to act as Stella's physician. He dropped Babs at home, wanting to go on to the hospital to check his patients. Babs then did something completely out of character. She called George Arthur's office.

"May I say who's calling?"

"This is his wife."

A pause. Of course the girl would recognize Stella's voice. "One moment, please."

"George Arthur speaking," an unmistakable voice said rather loudly some moments later. "Who is this?"

She eased the phone back onto its cradle. It was impossible for George Arthur to have returned to Fairland already. She and Louis had been on their way to their car when they ran into Stella and Roy Hunt and had driven directly—if not at breakneck speed—home.

Now that she was certain something quite out of the way was going on between Stella and Roy Hunt, Babs Poeglin never mentioned it again to Louis. She did not need him to share her suspicion. She didn't want him to, now that she realized it was true. More important, she was not certain what she herself really thought of Stella Arthur's behavior. There was the instinctive accusative reaction, of course. Wives were supposed to disapprove of other wives who were unfaithful. Not to do so would be to undermine the whole system of marital fidelity. But Babs's second reaction owed much to Claudia Cartwright's sermons.

Louis continued to attend services at the Presbyterian church, when he went. He had sat through several of Chet's sermons but had just shaken his head sadly when Babs asked what he thought.

"I'm just a simple country doctor," he said.

"That's why it's important to have a minister like that here. To wake us up."

When Chet was arrested in the bus depot, Louis might have crowed, but he didn't. The truth was he did not have much taste for gossip. The truth was that he was a boring man.

Claudia's sermons had altered the composition of the congregation, there was no doubt about that. Parishioners had been more or less evenly divided between men and women before Claudia, but in the several years of her pastorate the only men left were the bright-eyed ones who squirmed in their seats and exchanged knowing smiles with those around them during her sermons. What had happened to Babs, to use Claudia's language, was that her consciousness had been raised. She had never before thought that being a woman was a problem.

Once she put her mind to it, however, it was clear that Louis treated her as though she were an idiot. When was the last time they'd had an intelligent conversation?

"Isn't any conversation a sign of intelligence? Animals don't have conversations."

He did not even put down the medical journal he was reading when he said this. The little smile was in appreciation of what he thought was a witticism.

"Since I was a girl I have dreamed of going to New York, seeing some shows, eating in legendary places, staying in a luxury hotel."

He did look at her now. "Do you know what New York City is like in August?"

"August wouldn't be a good time to go in any case."

"But that's when I take my vacation."

"I could go with..." Her hand went out in a groping gesture. She really had not rehearsed this exchange. "Stella Arthur."

He laughed as if it were a joke. Babs said nothing, just sat there, waiting for him to finish. He stopped laughing and began to read again, but her silent presence began to have its effect. He put down his magazine.

"You're not serious."

"Why do you say that?"

"You want to go to New York without me?"

"Louis, I am an adult woman. I do not have to be squired and escorted wherever I go. Other women go places without their husbands."

"Stella Arthur?"

Why on earth had Stella's name popped out when she needed a possible traveling companion? It was obvious that Louis was at last remembering that elevator in Minneapolis. Babs said no more. She had ventured into dangerous waters and knew enough to move shoreward to safety.

That night, lying awake, Louis snoring in the bed next to hers, she imagined other ways the conversation might have gone. If only she had not mentioned Stella, for example. But she had blurted out Stella Arthur's name and that had ruined everything. She turned on her side and stared at the dull glow of the pulled shade and suddenly realized why Stella's name had occurred to her.

Of course. It was so obvious she actually blushed in the dark. Going away to New York represented, however unconsciously, an intention to sleep with someone other than Louis.

Behind her in the dark the steady sough of his snoring seemed a fading moral comment on that realization.

CLAUDIA CARTWRIGHT did not, of course, play bridge. It was the one thing about the pastor Babs Poeglin did not like. Claudia did crossword puzzles, which on any scale of trivial pursuits must rank well below bridge, or so at least Babs thought. Not that she cared to argue the matter. Liking bridge was not the result of a proof for her; she just liked to play and that was the end of it. Claudia, on the other hand, had an extended defense of crossword puzzles, which leaned rather heavily on the claim that all important people did them. But then she defined important people as those who did crossword puzzles.

"What is the church's stand on marital fidelity?"

Claudia's eyes slid past Babs and then came back. "The important question is what is your stand."

"I suppose it depends on the circumstances," Babs said, and she could imagine a shocked Louis reciting the relevant Commandment to her.

"Tell me about it." Claudia wore a loose smock-like coat in the parish office. She sat back, gripping the arms of her chair, receptive. It suddenly occurred to Babs that the pastor thought she was speaking of herself.

"It's not me!" she cried.

A gentle smile, as if this ploy had been anticipated.

Babs began to talk rapidly, words tumbling almost incoherently from her mouth, describing the meeting with Stella and Roy in the hotel elevator in Minneapolis, Stella's lie that her husband was there with them, her own inability to discuss it with Louis.

"Obviously it fascinates you."

Babs decided not to be put off by that. "Yes, it does."

"How old is Stella?"

"My age, maybe a year older."

"Making her..." Claudia said patiently.

"She certainly isn't forty."

"Ah."

Babs waved a hand dismissing Stella, and told Claudia of the conversation with Louis about New York.

"You should go," Claudia said firmly.

"That's what I think. But I don't want to fight about it."

Claudia's head tipped to the side. "That is a recipe for slavery, Barbara. What you should fear is that your husband will unwittingly hold you in contempt. Have I met him?"

"He's a Presbyterian."

Claudia shook her head. "I wish he could hear my sermons."

"So do I!"

"Bring him."

"My big mistake was mentioning Stella when I said I would go with someone else."

"Don't think of that as a mistake. Ask Stella if she would like to make the trip."

"But Louis remembers meeting them in Minneapolis."

"Remind Louis of his reaction when you said they were up to something."

Why hadn't she thought of that? Claudia must have been more than a match for her two husbands. At the moment she was single, but maybe you don't ever forget the techniques of spousal argument. The session ended with Babs promising Claudia she would broach the matter with Stella.

TELEPHONING STELLA and suggesting lunch would have been the most direct way to go about it, but Babs imagined herself in Stella's place and knew that such a call would alarm her. She would have to think of a less alarming approach.

At the bank, she went inside now, not using the drive-up window, wanting to catch at least a glimpse of Roy Hunt. Roy Hunt, of all people! She would have thought him duller than Louis, but his afternoon in a Minneapolis hotel with Stella had lent him the air of a complicated romantic figure. Provincial as Claudia no doubt would find it, Babs almost took pride in the fact that even in Fairland adultery of an interesting kind might occur.

Except that it was difficult really, really to believe that Stella had actually gone to bed with another man. In the abstract, in imaginative fantasy, anything was possible, but think of driving off with Roy Hunt on a day like today for a hotel room in Minneapolis. Babs began to feel a shared wickedness just dwelling on it.

The glimpse she caught of Roy was brief enough to feed her imaginings, but she still needed an excuse to get together with Stella. Ask her to bridge? If Stella were interested in duplicate, she would already be a regular at the Thursday afternoon game, and Babs certainly did not intend to bring an amateur.

It was amazing how things conspired to keep her mind on such matters. Claudia had given a lovely sermon on Emily Dickinson, and when Babs asked at the library for books on the poet, a librarian named Mabel mentioned several, among them one on Austin, Emily's brother.

"The strangest book," the woman said. She seemed to know a great deal. "Austin Dickinson for years had an affair with the wife of a friend, a woman Emily had known."

"I'd like to see it."

"It's engrossing, in its way, but maybe you'd want to begin with Weaver's life of Emily."

"Have you read the book about her brother?" Babs asked.

"Yes."

"Do you recommend it?"

"Let me put it this way. I'd be willing to read it again."

The book was certainly a revelation. Babs felt naive looking at the photographs in the book of nineteenth-century figures in long dresses and uncomfortable suits who had been far more modern than Babs Poeglin. And it wasn't because they had lived in the big city. Increasingly, Babs felt that she had wasted most of her life.

Mabel turned out to be an interesting woman. When Babs returned the book, she sought out the librarian and learned that she was only part-time. Babs came back on the Tuesday when Mabel would be there and they had a cup of coffee in the librarian's lounge.

"Do all librarians know so much about books?"

"My husband and I are book dealers."

"Where?"

"Right here in Fairland."

Babs couldn't believe it, not even when it became clear the store was out of town a ways, almost in the country. Well, as much in the country as the country club.

"Isn't it strange what can go on right under your nose and you don't see it?"

Mabel shrugged. "Used books are not everyone's thing."

"I'd like to come see the store."

"That's why it's there."

WHEN GEORGE Arthur was reported missing, Babs's first reaction was to stop looking for opportunities to get closer to Stella. The circumstances of his disappearance were such that she would not have trusted herself to talk with Louis about what had happened. Roy and George had been ice fishing and George had disappeared. Roy's speculation that George had drowned was treated with skepticism in the local paper; Babs did not understand why. The thought she scarcely dared allow to form in her mind would not go away. If Roy were in love with Stella he might have had a motive for wishing George dead.

But if it was hard to imagine people she knew having an affair, it was impossible to think of them involved in a murder. Well, not quite impossible. At first it had seemed impossible that Stella and Roy had spent the afternoon together in a Minneapolis hotel, but she would have had to be more naive than she was to doubt it. Imagine having a lover who would kill your husband in order to have you for himself.

With such thoughts in her mind she spoke to Stella one day when she was lunching with Claudia Cartwright at the country club, not a crowded place in winter. When she identified Stella for Claudia, the pastor said, "Introduce me."

"Oh I'm sure she's Episcopalian."

Claudia smiled an ecumenical smile. "Then she won't be surprised to meet a female pastor."

The introduction was a big flop and Babs didn't think it had to do with Claudia's clerical status. Or with the fact that she herself had been a year behind Stella in school. Claudia's jocular identification of herself as a "fisher of women as well as men" must have stirred painful memories.

"That woman is riddled with guilt," Claudia said, when they settled down to lunch. "I hate to think of her falling into the wrong hands."

"Guilt?"

Claudia sipped ice water as if drawing inspiration. "People have a habit of regarding misfortune as a divine punishment."

It seemed not to occur to Claudia that Stella might really be guilty. But then the pastor had a way of exonerating everyone but her former husbands of moral fault. It bothered Babs to think Stella might suppose she was some sort of religious fanatic. Not everyone understood Unitarianism. The next time she spoke to Stella, she would have to hint at her worldliness. Finally, the only one she discussed the matter with was Mabel Nicodemus.

Mabel's eyes lit up when Babs suggested Chinese food, and they met at the Great Wall of China, where the shrimp fried rice was out of this world, and talked books. It became a kind of habit and every few weeks they would go there. Twice Babs visited the bookstore, but it didn't interest her that much. She had never acquired the habit of buying books, the library was too convenient. Mabel didn't mind.

"Steve hates to let books go anyway," she said.

Her bearded husband was a pleasant man. Maybe the important thing about Mabel just then was that she was a happily married woman. So when George Arthur's disappearance came up, discussing it was different than it would have been with Claudia.

The original conversation took place over fried rice at The Great Wall, and it became a recurrent topic for them. Now that it was clear George Arthur was dead everyone wanted to know what had actually happened the day he disappeared.

"Drowning is the death I fear the most," Mabel said. "But under ice?"

"Imagine trying to come to the surface and bumping against a ceiling of ice." Babs shivered.

That was the tack they took those first times, before the body was found; how horrible it must have been to die that way. Mabel had not known either George or Roy so the conversation never got personal. Until Mabel met the widow, that is.

"We're buying her husband's books."

"She's getting rid of them so soon?"

"Can't wait."

"She can't need the money, Mabel."

"The books won't bring her all that much."

Mabel met Stella when she helped her husband box up the books.

"What did you think of her?"

"Pretty. I love her hair. How old is she?"

"My age."

"I wonder if she'll marry again."

"Stella has an eye for men," Babs said with authority.

"Oh?"

"I'll say no more."

Usually such a remark would have brought insistence that one go on, but Mabel accepted Babs's self-censorship. "I'll make sure she doesn't seduce my husband."

Babs laughed. Imagine that big teddy bear of a husband catching the eye of Stella Arthur.

SIX

When Roy asked if she had her key to the safe-deposit box, Stella said she did. It was in her jewelry box.

"Both of them?"

"The bank has the other one, doesn't it?" The customer had the key to one lock, the bank to the other, and both were necessary to open the box.

"You have two copies of yours."

Stella shook her head. "All I have is the one in my jewelry box. In a little red cardboard envelope."

"George must have kept the other one."

"I haven't seen it."

"Where would he be likely to put such a thing?"

"Roy, I don't think there were two keys. Maybe he put his in the safe in our bedroom." She hesitated. No need to tell Roy that neither of them had slept in the master bedroom for years, preferring other rooms and single beds. "But he knew where mine was."

Roy frowned and looked bewildered. "Stella, obviously I took care of everything myself. I gave George two keys, I distinctly remember that. And I mean two copies of the renter's key, one for him, one for you. That is quite standard when couples rent a box. He must have given you one and you put it in your jewelry box..."

"Roy! What in the name of God difference does it make?"

"As a banker I do not like the thought of a safe-deposit key unaccounted for."

"Could anyone come into the bank with a key and get into the box?"

Roy smiled patiently. "That is very unlikely. The first step is to sign one's name. The signature is compared with that on the application card. And of course one would have to know the name in the first place."

"We don't need the other key to open the box, do we?"

"Nooo."

"We will open the box and empty it and it doesn't matter that we don't have a third key, if such a key exists."

Honestly, she could slap Roy, he was so stubborn about this. Nothing she said seemed to have any effect on him.

"Indulge me, Stella. Where might he have put the key?"

"Roy, you are perfectly welcome to search the house. I am going out to the patio and wait for you there."

If that was her ultimatum, it left him unmoved. Stella went through the French doors to the patio and threw herself onto a padded lounge. She was trying to remember ever wishing she were free to marry Roy. What an impossible person he was. It was strange to think now that George had been in many ways, perhaps in most ways, a better man than Roy.

Of course these past months had taken their toll on both of them. Waiting all this time for George's body to be found, knowing it would be, having to pretend that it was at least possible he had just walked away that Tuesday, perhaps lost both his way and his mind, and was wandering somewhere unrecognized. Stella felt that she had finally gotten back her father's possessions but was prevented from laying final claim to them. It was during those months that she determined the library would be the first thing to go. That would be the first symbolic gesture toward reclaiming her inheritance.

Well, the books were gone, Rosemary had carted away the bookshelves, her father's billiard table had been brought from the company warehouse in which George had stored it, and Rosemary would make the billiard room exactly as it had been when her father was alive.

Roy came out on the patio and stared at her.

"What happened to the library?"

"It is going to be the billiard room again."

"But where are the books and shelves?"

"I sold them."

"Sold them! I can't believe it."

"It's true. They were a painful reminder of George."

That shut him up.

"I gather you did not find your precious key."

"No."

"Shall we go to the bank?"

He checked his watch. "In half an hour."

"Why wait?"

"There is no need for anyone else to see us open that box."

When they arrived at the bank it was clear that the business day was done. Roy pulled into his marked place. Roy Hunt, President. Did she want to be the wife of a banker? Odd that she had never really thought of Roy as a banker. There was one other car in the lot.

"Cowley," Roy explained.

The night watchman.

"Won't he think it odd, your bringing a customer in after hours?"

"No. I told him yesterday I'd be doing this. I invoked his confidence. He will be expecting to see a very upset widow. It would help if you could cry. The idea is that this is a devastating enough task for you, but to do it in public with witnesses..."

It turned out that she did feel sad when they went inside. Cowley turned a big wide face on her, his eyes swimming with sympathy. The Widow Arthur. That is what she was now, the bereaved wife, her husband of so many years cruelly dead. And she herself had been put through the torture of a three-month wait. Stella began to feel genuinely sorry for herself and tears rose easily to her eyes.

The guard opened the stainless steel gate and the door beyond and then they were inside the safe-deposit box area. Roy nodded significantly to Cowley who withdrew. Roy held out his hand. Stella unsnapped the red cardboard envelope, shook the flat key into her palm, and offered it to Roy.

He needed the little stepladder to reach the level at which the box was. The place reminded Stella of a post office. He slid a flat key from a ring of similar keys sideways into a lock and then took the key Stella had given him and put it in the matching lock. He turned one, then the other, and slowly lifted the molded steel door to reveal the green metal box within. He slid it out and came gingerly down the stepladder.

After he had placed the box on the table in the center of the room, he checked the door through which they had come from the main part of the bank. Satisfied, he returned to the box. He nodded to Stella.

"Open it." In his voice was the musical promise of an adult speaking to a child at Christmas.

One third of the top of the box was hinged. Stella lifted it slowly, looking at Roy. He came close beside her. When the lid was back and the inside of the box revealed Roy gasped.

"It's empty!" Stella cried.

Roy actually turned the box over to see if it had a false bottom. He wheeled and ran back to the step-ladder, scrambled up it, and stood on tiptoe to peer into the cavity from which the box had been taken. Stella watched him, stunned. After all this—she was so confused she did not know what "this" was, but it was the memory of that dreadful Tuesday, the strain of the months of waiting, everything—after all this, nothing.

Roy looked down at her, his mouth open. "I don't understand."

"Have you got the right box?"

The question gave him a moment's hope, but it died as soon as it appeared in his eyes. How could he be mistaken about a thing like that?

How long did they remain in there trying to adjust to the fact that they had come for hundreds of thousands of dollars and found an empty box? When they did emerge, Cowley stepped back respectfully and they went right out to Roy's car. He started the engine and drove out of the lot, but Stella doubted he knew what he was doing.

He drove back to the house in silence, got out of the car, and strode toward the door. Stella hurried after him.

"Roy, what is it?"

He looked around the living room, then slapped his forehead with his open palm. "Where the hell is that other key?"

"Roy, maybe that's the explanation. Someone had the other key and got to the box before us. They've had months to do it."

He nodded. "But who could have it?" He looked wildly about as if he expected an answer. He peered at her. "Do you know what my first thought was?"

"What?"

"George never wanted to put his money in that box. He did, or pretended to, but he never trusted me or the bank to protect that money from the IRS."

"We should have checked the box right away."

Everything they thought of was like that: if sensible, thought of too late. What might have been. It did not help to feel like such a damned fool. Even searching the house made Stella feel that somewhere George was having the last laugh. Their plans and schemes were ridiculous in light of what had happened. Had they really thought George was that stupid? Put all your money in Roy's bank, in a hidden deposit box. If George had trusted banks he would have come up with some variation of Roy's plan long before.

Upstairs, carefully going through the contents of the wall safe in the master bedroom, Stella took comfort from the insurance policies there. And she must not forget that she had inherited all of Arthur Enterprises. Arthur Enterprises! Very soon now they would become Larson Enterprises again. Roy didn't share her relief at the thought.

"George didn't tell you much about his business dealings, did he?"

"I think I had a pretty good idea of what was going on," Stella said testily.

"Then you know about the borrowing."

Stella sat on a corner of the bed. "Tell me."

George had taken large loans at all the local banks, borrowing on the companies that made up his empire. It was Roy's understanding that he had gone to the city as well in quest of money.

"What for?"

"To expand."

"Expand what? Where?"

Roy sank into a boudoir chair. The expression he had had when he saw the empty safe-deposit box was back on his face.

"If I didn't know better, I would say it was his way of liquidating everything. Selling off. Getting it in cash."

"But why?"

Roy had no answer to that, but of course she was not really asking him. Her husband had suddenly become a stranger to her. Throughout their marriage she had seen him as an obstacle to her happiness and the usurper of her father's wealth. Now, stunned by this turn of events, she wanted Roy out of the house. She had to think this through.

"We've got to keep looking, Stella."

"If it's here it won't go away. I don't think there is any key."

"I hope you're wrong."

For the first time since George drowned, Roy kissed her. Stella permitted it, if only to hurry him on his way, but how meaningless it was, his lips on hers, his hands squeezing her arms. He closed his eyes but she stared at the thicket of his eyebrow as he pressed his mouth to hers. She went downstairs with him and saw him to his car. Watching him go off down the driveway, she felt she had somehow drifted out of the human race.

She mixed a pitcher of Manhattans and sat in the billiard room with the lights off—sat in the leather chair that had been her father's and tried to sort out the thoughts that had begun upstairs.

Why would George have wanted to realize as much cash as he could from the business? Had he been intending to leave her?

She tried to dismiss the thought as ironic. All these years she had been tolerating George, but what if he had tired of *her?* The irony was that she would not have noticed.

Had he found out about her and Roy? From whom? She hardly needed to ask. That hotel elevator in Minneapolis had prompted her and Roy to decide to get rid of George. If the Poeglins had told him, he might have decided the same thing. First, get as much cash as he could, then enter into divorce proceedings on the basis of the pittance left.

Thank God he hadn't thought of just killing her.

She shook her head. If George had suspected anything, would he have agreed to that ridiculous ice-fishing invitation?

The truth is she had not really known George. Because she hadn't wanted to. Roy knew more about her husband's business dealings than she did. For all she knew, George could have fallen passionately in love and decided to leave her. With the money he had apparently gathered together, he could have been planning to abscond with his new love.

She sipped her drink carefully. If there was some-one George meant to go off with, that someone would have known of the money. With George disappeared, the woman could have fled with the money. If not then, now when it was clear George was dead.

By her third drink, Stella had developed a compli-cated possible account of what had happened. George and his new love had decided to milk the company dry and go off and start a new life. The woman had been sent on ahead, perhaps to Switzerland, to get the money into a safe account. George was to join her. Meanwhile, she and Roy plot to kill George and sub-merge him beneath the frozen lake. The woman waits and waits. She will get word of George's disappear-ance and think he is coming. But he does not come. She is confused. These past months have been hell for her too. Now she knows her lover will never come, but she has all that money with which to console herself.

Stella went on spinning this tale to herself. It would have become more elaborate, but she stopped, and what stopped her was a far simpler explanation. One right before her eyes.

Roy.

What if it was Roy, not George, who had betrayed her?

She had only his word that the money had been put into that safe-deposit box. Of course he would have made the fuss he did about the missing copy of the key. That was *before* they discovered the money was missing. But he was simply building a case. Then rac-ing back here and insisting they ransack the house in search of a nonexistent key.

Night fell, Stella was drunk now, yet her mind seemed oddly clear. Her emotions were numb.

The key provided a possible variation. George had put the money in the box, but Roy gave him only one renter's key, retaining the other for himself. That meant that at any time during the past four and a half months, Roy could have emptied the box.

All that her thinking did, it seemed, was to give her a choice as to who had betrayed her.

But she was certain now the traitor was Roy Hunt.

SEVEN

MABEL AND Dr. Poeglin's wife were beside the pool drinking iced tea. Seated at his desk in the bookstore, Steve Nicodemus could hear the faint murmur of their voices on the summer air. A buzz of gnats by comparison with the thunderclap of an errant golf ball banging against the metal wall of the bookstore. The stand of trees at the end of his property suggested a forest primeval stretching on into the west, but actually the woods were only twenty yards deep. Beyond were the pampered grounds of the Fairland Country Club. Every week or so in summer Steve gathered up the golf balls at the back of the building and by September he had several pails full, which he sold to a driving range on the far side of town.

Nicodemus slid open the top drawer of his desk, pushed aside some old letters, and unearthed two identical red cardboard envelopes. It had been two weeks since one of them had fallen from the book he had bought from Mrs. Arthur. The other contained his key to the safe-deposit box at the first Southeastern of Minnesota bank in which he and Mabel kept their wills, insurance policies, and savings certificates. She had an envelope just like it.

It did not tax his imagination to think this key would open a world of wealth. Of course he could not use it. He could not saunter into the bank and scrawl George Arthur's signature and expect to be led back to the safe-deposit area and have the box opened for him. It wasn't that he couldn't imitate Arthur's signature. Samples of it were available in the man's books. Nicodemus had actually tried writing it, filling several pages with his attempts. With practice he could produce an identical signature, he was sure of it.

Of course this was all a kind of dangerous daydreaming. What risk would he actually run if he did that? Is it a crime to sign the name of a dead person? It certainly would not be an innocent act to try to get into another person's safe-deposit box. To be caught doing such a thing would be the end of him as a businessman. There was no way he could live down such a deed. A deed that might not be worth the risk anyway.

Oh, he didn't believe that. If George Arthur had a safe-deposit box, it would contain something so valuable he did not want it at home or in his office. Nicodemus was certain that if the contents of that box were his, his life would never be the same again.

Another female voice became audible outside and Nicodemus got to his feet as if this would improve his hearing. At first he could not place the voice, but then he had it. Rosemary Burnet. He slipped into his loafers and started toward the front door. Before he reached it, it was pushed open and the bell above it set jangling.

Rosemary entered, looking up at the bell. Just as the tinkling died away there was an explosive sound from the back of the store.

"What in God's name was that?"

"A golf ball."

Her nose wrinkled in the way he remembered. Clearly she thought he was joking. He explained about the country club.

"Of course! Coming out this road, I didn't think of that. I wonder if any of my drives have bonged against your wall like that."

"It takes a serious mistake to do that."

"You don't know me very well, do you?"

"I don't know you at all. What can I show you? I'm afraid I don't have much in interior decorating."

"I wouldn't look at it if you did. Just show me around."

Military and regional history did not detain them, nor did philosophy and theology, though she showed some interest in the psychology section until she leafed through a few turgid tomes.

"Literature is in the back."

When they went through the open area where his desk was, he noticed that the red cardboard envelopes were quite visible on the desk. He felt a wave of unease when he thought that one of those envelopes had fallen out of her uncle's book.

"You had room for all George's books?"

"Oh they're not unpacked yet."

A little smile of complicity. "I put the bookshelves in the warehouse. I hope I find a use for them. I can see they wouldn't be right here. These steel shelves are much more serviceable."

"Have you been at work on the billiard room?"

"There's no work involved. The point is to make the room match the photographs Stella has of it from when her father was alive. I can let myself go only on the sitting room and sun porch." She shrugged. "The only reason I'm doing it is as a favor to Aunt Stella."

"And someday it will all be yours?"

She smiled. "That's my line. I certainly wouldn't move to Fairland. Don't you miss Minneapolis?"

"I think Mabel may. I see enough of it when I go up on buying trips."

"When do you plan to unpack George's books?"

"Maybe your aunt will buy them back."

"I'll help you get started if you like."

Her expression did not suggest that her remark had any ulterior meaning, but it made him uneasy again.

"Is there something in particular that interests you?"

She laughed. "Like I told Stella that day you were there, George once opened a book and it was full of money. Why don't we check one?"

He was almost relieved at the suggestion. He flipped open the carton beside his desk, pulled out one of George Arthur's books, and handed it to Rosemary. She held it closed between her hands and looked at him.

"It reminds me of looking for direction in a random passage of the Bible."

"Open it."

She opened it on her lap and fanned the pages. Nothing.

"Want to try another?"

"Next time. Look me up when you're in Minneapolis." She took a card from her purse and dealt it onto the desk.

He offered her coffee and they sat in the office area, chatting about Minneapolis. Zeno decided that Rosemary deserved attention and jumped up beside her to be petted. How old was Rosemary? In her thirties somewhere, more than a quarter of a century younger than he was, but for the first time in years he found himself in the classic situation in which male and female of the species circle one another speculatively. On the shelf behind his left ear was a first edition of William Dean Howells's *Indian Summer,* a delightful tale of an older man's infatuation with a young girl. And vice versa. He was almost relieved when Mabel came in to the tinkling of bells and the conversation turned to Minneapolis reminiscences.

THE SAFE-DEPOSIT key in the red cardboard envelope had immobilized him. He did not unpack George Arthur's books. Neither did he, as he told himself half a dozen times a day he should, return the key to Mrs. Arthur. This sensible resolution was undermined by considerations that would have delighted a Pharisee. He had bought the books and whatever the books contained was now his. He thought of other things he had come upon in secondhand books—letters, photographs, newspaper clippings. Didn't they belong to him? Moreover, if someone bought a book from his shelves, would he not concede that whatever they might find in the book was also theirs? This had actually happened. A customer came back and told him there had been an old World War II savings bond in a copy of *Mrs. Miniver* bought from the Nicodemus Bookstore.

"It's yours," he had said.

"Don't you want to know how much it's worth?"

"It doesn't matter."

The man told him anyway and Nicodemus knew a moment of regret. But he had not claimed any of the money. If he was damn fool enough not to leaf through a book before he put it on the shelf, that was his problem. The customer, a retired schoolteacher named Owens, pressed the point.

"But what if I found it when I was just browsing here and slipped it into my pocket?"

Nicodemus, having taken the high ground, decided to stay there. "How can I be robbed of something I don't know I own?"

There was something wrong with that logic, he knew it then, but he was suffused with altruistic righteousness in saying it, and that seemed to make up for having accidentally enriched Owens. From that time on he had checked every book he bought before putting it on the shelf.

These considerations favored the view that the key was his. The laws of salvage, he was sure, would bear out his claim. But these arguments did not touch the matter of his using the key to get into someone else's safe-deposit box. This realization rendered all the rest of it pointless and convinced him that he should return the key. There was no doubt of it. But still he did not do it.

Soon after Rosemary's visit he went to the bank and through the procedure of opening his own box. The woman who waited on him had a weak chin, an overbite, and extremely stylish eyeglasses. A plastic name tag told him her name was Phyllis. Had she ever waited on him before? If so, she gave no sign of it, waiting with a toothy smile while he filled out the slip, taking it and making certain it was properly filled out, checking his signature against that in a little file card box she brought out from beneath the counter, putting the slip back in the folder, and then turning to him.

"If you will follow me, Mr. Nicodemus."

The gates were swung open but she had to push through the door. She had to check a chart to figure out where the box was located. He was about to tell her, but decided to let this run its natural course. Finally she knew where to go.

"You have your key?"

He handed it to her.

"I should have asked you that before we came in."

"Not used to this?"

She shook her head. "I had to get away from a window. I spent sixteen years as a teller and I needed a change."

"I looked at it to remember the number before I filled out the slip. I thought you had seen it then."

She was grateful for the suggestion that she had not made a mistake in the procedure. After she used her key and his and got down his box, she asked if he wished to be alone.

"I'll use one of the rooms."

There were three windowless rooms along the wall, scarcely larger than phone booths, in which the minor Midas could contemplate his wealth. Nicodemus went into the middle one, closed the door, and sat at the counterlike desk with his safe-deposit box before him. What would he do?

He pulled the box toward him and slowly lifted the lid. Its contents were familiar, but he was imagining unimaginable surprises. Stocks, bonds, whatever—he would lift them from the box and put them into the inner pockets of his corduroy jacket. It would be that simple. Then he would call Phyllis back and have her put the box away, take his key, and walk out.

The major difficulty that remained was that he did not know the number of George Arthur's box. He looked at the little red envelope that had fallen out of one of George Arthur's books, half tempted to drop it into the wastebasket. But what he did was slip it into his own safe-deposit box.

He remained in the room for several minutes and then summoned Phyllis. After she put the box away and gave him back his key, she waited and left the room with him. At the counter, he stopped and smiled vaguely over Phyllis's head.

"Let me see my registration card. I'm trying to remember how long I've had this box."

She reached under the counter, brought forth the file box, and pushed it to him. He ran his finger over the first cards, looking for Arthur, George. It was not there. He went on to his own, pulled it out, frowned at it, shook his head, and returned it. Before pushing the box back to Phyllis, he checked the A's again. There was no box registered under George Arthur.

"Everything okay?"

Nicodemus turned to face Mr. Roy Hunt, the president of the bank.

"All through," Steve managed to say.

Hunt smiled at Phyllis, nodded to Steve, turned away. Phyllis looked at him and smiled, as if she had just passed a test. It was all Steve could do not to run out of the bank. He felt he had been caught in the act. All the way home he wished he had that goddamn key with him. He would have thrown it in the river to be rid of it.

Back in his office, he felt almost liberated from his obsessive thoughts about that damned key. It was a key to nothing as far as he was concerned, and the first chance he had he would give it back . . .

Back to Mrs. Arthur? But why assume the key had belonged to her husband? Perhaps George Arthur too had bought the key along with the book. No. But if he had simply rented the box, why not assume his wife had a key to it as well? Relief rushed in upon him and he could have kicked himself for not thinking of this immediately. He took Zeno onto his lap and ran his hand repeatedly over his black coat. Within minutes, speculation began again.

So what if Stella Arthur had a duplicate key? He had the other and he could empty the box. Mrs. Arthur would have no reason to remove the contents of the box. If she knew of it, if she had a key. From what he could guess of the relationship between the Arthurs, from the fact that the key had been hidden in a book, he could believe that George had not told her of the box. That would make it all the more interesting. What had he stashed away there, a secret from his wife?

He stopped himself. He had to get his mind once and for all off this stupid subject. He needed to break his routine.

"I'm going to Minneapolis tomorrow," he told Mabel when he went into the house. "Want to come along?"

"I work at the library tomorrow."

"Take a day off."

"Steve, I really don't want to go to Minneapolis."

So he went alone.

EIGHT

ROSEMARY CONSIDERED herself to be as much a widow as her Aunt Stella, but of course she didn't expect anyone else to think of her as one. Who even remembered Russ now, except maybe Beatrice? But for Rosemary those long ago days of love were as vivid as her memories of Uncle George. Alone with her thoughts she could never really believe that she was now in her thirty-third year.

Thirty-two her last birthday, this was her thirty-third year. It made it even more incredible to think of it that way. How could Russ's fiancée be so old?

Russ, of course, remained forever young. He had gone off to Vietnam at twenty-four and never come back. The dead do not grow older. Losing him, the only man she had ever really loved, had made Rosemary's life seem posthumous when it did not seem unreal. At the time the awful news came she had been waiting for Russ, and she had gone on doing that ever since, knowing he would never come back. She hadn't lost her mind or anything, she simply made this futile waiting the definition of her life.

Undramatically. She stopped talking about Russ to other people as soon as she gave up hope that the news was wrong. Her memories were her own and she had no desire to share them with others. But oh what lovely memories they were.

They had met on the campus of the University of Minnesota. He was a graduate student, she was majoring in art. Everyone had advised her to go to Walker, she didn't need a university degree to be an artist, but that made her aim seem more exclusive than it was. Besides, the advice suggested that she was some kind of dummy who couldn't meet university requirements.

Maybe she was overcompensating by taking so many courses in history and political science, but thank God she had. That is how she met Russ. He was a teaching assistant in classical political theory who seemed to have memorized Aristotle the way some people memorize the Bible.

"Oh, I did that too. Wanna test me?"

"How?"

"Ask me Mark fourteen-twenty-five."

"Okay. Mark fourteen-twenty-five." She had no idea what it meant.

"Amen I say to thee I shall not drink again the fruit of the vine until the day I drink new wine in the kingdom of heaven."

"How do I know you're right?"

"Don't you believe in inerrancy?"

He had been raised a southern Baptist and had been attracted north by a graduate student stipend. He was half a head taller than Rosemary so when she was with him she didn't wear heels much, which was all right with her. Dates were largely a matter of talking over coffee for hours in Bridgeman's, just being together. His stipend did little more than keep the wolf from the door.

"That's what you need."

"Money?"

"Something to keep the wolf from the door." He leered. Even his leer was nice.

"That's my father's job."

Her dad liked Russ. Who wouldn't? They talked Twins and Vikings and agreed to disagree about Dallas. Her mother thought he was too thin but not even malted milk and beer could fatten him up. Not that he drank beer.

"I'm a teetotaler."

"Nothing wrong with that," her father said, but he sounded as though he couldn't think of much right about it either.

Once, after listening to her parents tell her what a nice boy he was, Rosemary tried to think of flaws in Russ's character, but all she could come up with was that he was too nice to people. People took advantage of him. He did the lion's share of assistant work for the world-class professor who lectured them twice a week, leaving exams and questions to his five assistants. Russ made up the questions for the exams, was always available to students, but refused to complain.

"Rosie, it isn't work. I love this. I want to be a teacher. This is what it is."

That made sense, of course, but the other assistants wanted to be professors too.

He had taken all but one of his candidacy exams. The plan was to take that, write his dissertation, and go on the job market. Two years more at most.

There was something else he was, a patriot, and when the Vietnam War heated up, Russ volunteered. He was exempt as a graduate student, but he dismissed that fact as an irrelevancy. Where he came from men fought their country's battles without complaint. He was genuinely puzzled by student reaction to the war. Rosemary sometimes wondered whether he would have joined the marines if there hadn't been all that demonstrating. There were tears in his eyes when some students burned the American flag.

The marines were a family tradition, almost a southern tradition. His enlistment made Rosemary realize that she agreed with him rather than with the protesting students. Most of them were just imitating their leaders, but that was no excuse. It wasn't a matter of my country right or wrong. Russ went off to an ambiguous war because he thought his country was in the right. He still thought so in the last letter he wrote her, a letter that arrived after the news that he had been killed.

When she met the bearded book dealer in Aunt Stella's house in Fairland she had the eeriest feeling that, despite his age and the beard, he was a kind of reincarnation of Russ. That is how Russ would have looked if he had lived to become a professor, lived to be as old as Nicodemus. How old was that? Late fifties, more or less. Russ would have been in his late thirties if he had lived. It was that sense of finding her past in the present that led her to visit the bookstore in Fairland.

She supposed one of the two women sitting by the pool must be Mrs. Nicodemus, but it wasn't clear which until Mabel came into the bookstore. Sitting there talking with the two of them, Rosemary imagined that this was how it might have been with Russ and her. Oh, not a bookstore, but being at ease together and talking books. She had the sense the Nicodemuses had set out to do something and were doing it and it was exactly what they had hoped it would be.

"Getting the pension first was important," Mabel said. "And I've always worked part-time."

"Pension?"

"Steve was a fireman in Minneapolis for twenty years."

He wasn't offended when she laughed, but she would have given anything if she had been able to repress that instinctive reaction to the notion that a twenty-year apprenticeship as a fireman had been served in order to have this bookstore in Fairland.

She apologized when Mabel went outside to the pool.

"It is kind of funny."

"The nicest man I ever knew went into the marines."

"I was in the marines."

"You were!"

"Before I was a fireman." His beard adjusted itself to his smile. "Just at the time the war ended. I was seventeen when I enlisted."

"He was twenty-four."

"An officer?"

She shook her head. "Just a grunt. That's what he wanted. He died in Vietnam."

He just nodded. It was the first time she had mentioned Russ in ten years.

"Were you engaged?"

"Yes."

Would he laugh if he knew they had never made love? Russ may not have remained the full-tilt Baptist he had once been but in his book you did not sleep with a woman until you married her.

"Then let's marry now," she had whispered.

"I leave in two days."

Two hours would have been heaven. He wavered, but did not agree. When he left she was still a virgin, waiting for the return of her one true love. She had tried to wish she had broken down his resistance, led him on to make love to her, but that would have been a bitter rather than a consoling memory, to have made him do something wrong.

"I thought Baptists didn't believe in nuns," she had taunted him.

"What do you know about Baptists?"

It was heaven to be held by him and hell to realize he was going away. Would they have acted differently if they had known they would never see one another again? The answer of course was no. But with Stephen Nicodemus she thought she had a sense of what it would have been like to grow old with Russ.

"How's your aunt?"

"I haven't seen her yet this trip. She sounds awful on the phone."

"She's been through a lot."

Rosemary didn't think Stella really mourned the death of her husband. That was awful to think, perhaps, but her aunt and uncle had never been close.

"Ours is what was once called a marriage of convenience," Stella had told her once when Rosemary realized her aunt and uncle slept in separate rooms.

"For whom?"

Stella laughed, almost merrily. "That is a very good question." But she had put a hand on Rosemary's arm and, her eyes still bright from laughing, said, "Don't think that I'm unhappy, sweetheart."

Actually Rosemary had been thinking of Uncle George. As far as Rosemary understood the situation, George had rescued Stella's father's business and taken her into the bargain. The business had flourished but he seemed to have done less well with his wife.

Rosemary had come to Fairland this time at the invitation of Beatrice, an old Minneapolis friend who had moved there and become her uncle's secretary. When she left the bookstore at three in the afternoon, she urged Nicodemus again to look her up the next time he came to Minneapolis. Not that she was going right back. Whatever Beatrice wanted would come up at dinner the following night. And right now she intended to stop by the country club to see if Stella was there.

As she was saying goodbye there was another crash in the back of the store.

"Another?"

He groaned. "Golf is a very long season."

"Is there a shortcut to the country club from here?"

"I'm not the one to ask."

When Mabel got up from a deck chair and came to the fence to say goodbye, Rosemary commented on what a wonderful life the two of them led.

"I really don't miss Minneapolis."

"Why should you, with the life you have?"

She drove back to town and took Country Road B west; when she finally pulled into the country club it took an act of faith to think that the Nicodemus Bookstore was only one stray golf shot away.

It had been years since she had played this course, but there had been a time when she vacationed in Fairland as her aunt's guest, and many days had been spent at the country club, playing tennis, golfing, but above all golfing. Stella didn't golf. Had that been the reason Rosemary preferred it? What an odd thought, but not without truth.

As she came onto the veranda of the clubhouse, her name was called and she smiled without recognition at the man who rose from a table and came toward her.

"Rosemary? Roy Hunt. An old friend of your uncle's. He banked with us."

Rosemary nodded. It seemed an odd identification.

"Is Stella with you?"

"Then she's not here?" Rosemary surprised herself answering a question with a question. She recognized it as a ploy of her aunt's.

"I haven't seen her. I'm told you're redecorating the house."

Rosemary nodded. She was about to turn away when she realized who he was.

"You were with him, weren't you? With Uncle George. The two of you were ice fishing together."

"That's right."

"Would you think me gruesome if I asked you to tell me exactly what happened that day?"

"Well . . ." He stepped back, frowning.

Just so she had thought she wanted someone to tell her exactly how Russ had died, but there was no one who could. None of his squad had survived. Not that George and Russ were the same thing, but still, she would like in a nonmorbid way to know precisely how her uncle had died. Stella was very vague about it.

Roy Hunt seemed to regret having greeted her. The account he gave her of the accident was no more satisfactory than Stella's. Maybe it was morbid to want to know all the details of someone's death. Someone. Uncle George was a someone, but Russ was infinitely more. And she would never know what his last moments were like.

She did not detain Roy Hunt when he got up to go back to his table.

NINE

Roy Hunt had three gin and tonics in him when he accosted Rosemary on the veranda of the country club and he felt like a damned fool when he reeled back to the table where Jimmy Rowan awaited him. Jim had won the state lottery, dropped out of medical school, joined the club, and dedicated his life to drink. Roy did not like Jimmy's smile.

"No luck, Roy?"

"That is Stella Arthur's niece," Roy said, sitting forward as if to negate the taunting remark. But the gin and tonics were not so easily deflected. He looked sternly at Jimmy. "She wanted to talk about her uncle."

"How is the grieving widow?"

Jimmy seemed determined to be obnoxious, something he could pull off with ease. The crack about Rosemary had been uncalled-for, but looking across the table at Jimmy, Roy was reminded of that afternoon in Minneapolis when he and Stella had bumped into the Poeglins, and the memory made him feel as guilty now as he had then. More important, it induced caution. Lips pressed tightly together, Roy inhaled deeply through his nose.

"It's no easy thing for a woman suddenly to find herself alone."

Jimmy hummed and looked out toward the practice green.

"Fortunately, there is a good deal of business that simply has to be transacted, sorry or not. Because of that I have seen her several times during this difficult period and I must say I marvel at the way she's holding up."

"All that waiting," Jimmy said, dipping toward him. "That would have driven me mad."

Roy nodded. His hand went out for his drink but he stopped it. Thinking of Stella and the remarkable way she was getting through this made him feel like a jackass. Jimmy was currently picking fruit out of his glass, all that remained of his whiskey sour, and Roy felt for him the contempt one drinker feels for another.

"Shock," Jimmy said, nibbling on a cherry. "Nature numbs us in adversity and that helps us get through it."

"In varying degrees," Roy said. Whatever was numbing Jimmy Rowan was not nature.

"Nature and art," Jimmy went on, ignoring him. "She should take tranquilizers."

"What kind?" Roy asked sharply, but Jimmy held up a hand that from heel to tip of middle finger, must have been ten inches high.

"I wish I hadn't mentioned that."

That Jimmy might have become a doctor was a sobering thought. Two years of medical school and the man knew what was best for Stella Arthur as if he were privy to all her secrets. It was a good thing he wasn't. Stella herself espoused some secular version of Christian Science: the only healer is Nature herself. Agreeing with her seemed a way of cutting through the smug cloud that enveloped the former medical student. But

Jimmy had caught a waiter's eye and was pointing significantly to his empty glass.

"Having another, Roy?" he asked when the waiter came.

Roy shook his head firmly. At the moment he felt like a man who had had his last gin and tonic. Vague vistas of sobriety and moral superiority beckoned him, and he was depressed by the thought of himself sitting on this veranda with Jimmy Rowan.

"I may play the back nine," he announced.

"When?"

"Now. The light will hold. I could play nine in an hour and a half, two hours at most. Then, a shower, dinner..." Roy smiled. He liked the prospect, not least because Jimmy was frowning disapproval.

"Better have another gin and tonic and relax," Jimmy advised. He made it sound like a prescription.

"Most doctors would insist on exercise."

"Who's your doctor?"

"A man in Minneapolis." Somehow this lie chased the last vestige of guilt he had felt when he remembered running into the Poeglins. But when he stood, Jimmy looked up at him with half-closed eyes.

"Going back and forth to Minneapolis must be good exercise."

Maybe he would think of a response to that later, but at the moment he felt as if it were Jimmy Rowan who had surprised them in that elevator. Roy nodded farewell and, conscious of the effort it took, walked a straight line across the veranda and then went inside and headed for the locker room.

In the steamy room, filled with the boisterous sounds of bonhomie and men in varying stages of undress, Roy changed into golf clothes, and in the pro shack was advised to play the front nine.

"Look at that." Quinn the pro pointed at the first tee. Not a soul in sight. "Play as a singleton. I'll look the other way."

Roy ignored the suggestion that it was at Quinn's sufferance he played alone. On the first tee, he hurried his drive to ensure that he would not be robbed of his solitary round by the arrival of other late golfers. His ball was a pop-up that went a hundred yards, but he piled into the cart, depressed the pedal, and was on his way.

The first fairway, no matter what kind of drive he had hit, never failed to seem the entry into a wholly different world, one in which decisions were always crystal clear, good and bad infallibly connected with results, all other cares nonexistent. Roy Hunt golfed twice a week at most, and when he was not on the course he seldom thought of the game, but once he donned golf shoes and his billed cap with the logo of the country club on it, the fortunes of the game constituted his universe.

He reached his ball, got out, eased it into a better lie with the toe of his three wood, looked back to the still empty first tee, and took three practice swings. Roy Hunt's golf swing, viewed from within his mind and imagination, and as it appeared to the objective observer, was two wholly different things. In his mind's eye, he saw the club head being taken away from the ball in an easy arc, his left elbow unbent. When the club shaft was behind his head and parallel to the ground, there was a fraction of a second pause and then he brought it around in an accelerating but deliberate motion during which his body weight shifted from right to left. Club met ball, but seconds after contact his head was still down, eyes trained on the ground before him. In fact, he jerked the club up, came down on the ball with a chopping motion that was all arms and no body, and was looking hopefully down the fairway almost before the ball was hit. Quinn the pro wisely discouraged the use of videotape by members interested in improving their golf. The examined game is not worth playing, as an old Greek golfer must have said.

If enjoyment of golf depended on excellence of play, the links of the nation would be empty, fairway grass gone to seed, and sand traps aflower with hardy weeds. Like millions of others, Roy Hunt thought that with practice and more play his game would improve dramatically. What he liked to consider his typical game was actually an ideal he had never reached. So he was not angry when his second shot landed in a fairway bunker and his first attempt to get it out of there sent up a spray of sand that left the ball unmoved. Out of compassion for the ground crew, he threw his ball onto the fairway, took a five iron, and hit the best shot of the season, sending the ball on a clean line to the green where it rolled to within feet of the pin. What he wouldn't have given to be playing with others when he hit that ball!

For the next three holes he played extremely well, uncharacteristically well, but far from increasing the psychological distance between his game and the real world, he became disturbed by a possibility that, once admitted to his mind, refused to be expelled. His cart slowed to less than walking pace.

Stella was the love of his life, had been since high school. Not even her marriage to George Arthur had changed that. He considered them married to each other so far as the courts of heaven were concerned and that is how Stella saw it too. When they met to make love, it was as if they were asserting her true status rather than violating it. Nonetheless, running into the Poeglins had scared the hell out of both of them.

Why? The thought that now lodged itself in Roy's mind was that the basic reason was Stella's fear George would divorce her and keep the lion's share of what she still considered her father's wealth.

If Stella had not cared about money, she would have married him, not George. The whole motivation for her marriage was money.

He tried to shake the chilling thought away. Put like that, it made the whole business seem more crass than it was. Stella saw herself as protecting what her father had achieved. Her life was that of an incredibly loyal daughter.

But the loyalty was centered on money, there was no way to deny it. Roy Hunt did not disdain money. As a banker, he understood the role money plays in the lives of human beings. There was nothing wrong in his book with Stella's interest in money.

To protect what she had sacrificed their love to, they had decided to get rid of George after the unsettling meeting with the Poeglins in Minneapolis. So they had arranged his death. Killed him. Murdered him. For money. If anyone else knew what they had done, the description of the deed would be harsh. Wife and lover murder husband in order to take over his estate.

Would their roles be seen as equal? Disconcerting thoughts assailed him. Stella had been along on the ice-fishing expedition, but what if she should deny knowing anything about it? His own safety, he realized, was in Stella's hands. If she should ever turn on him, he was doomed, but was she equally at risk? Such questions could only arise by putting aside their lifelong love, but when he put it aside for purposes of speculation, he realized he had no security at all. Stella, if she denied everything, was not similarly vulnerable.

Standing over his putt on the fourth green, he thought of the empty safe-deposit box and became a statue. Empty! After everything he had done, to open the box and find in it nothing at all. What a trick George had played on him if he had only seemed to acquiesce in the idea of the unlisted box and then cleaned it out at the first opportunity.

If it was George who emptied it. But who else could it have been? He straightened, tapped his ball distractedly, and as it rolled unerringly into the hole, said aloud, "Stella."

From that point on, his game fell apart. He sprayed the ball into every point on the compass. On the fifth hole, he lost two balls in the lake before he managed to loft one into the marsh grass on the far side. The wheels of his cart sank in the spongy ground and he did not dare stop. He dropped another ball onto the fairway and went on.

Imagine that sometime during those terrible months of waiting, Stella had emptied the box of those seven hundred and fifty thousand dollars. She could have opened an account in Minneapolis, buried the money in the backyard, put it in the safe in the master bedroom, anything! It was the thought of that cash rather than the supposed Arthur estate, that enabled Roy to do what he had done at Lake Owatonna. Stella obviously did not know that the development of the shopping mall was a gamble on which George had bet everything. Roy himself could bring the whole Arthur empire tumbling down on the basis of loans his bank had made, and there were other, more ruthless lenders who were now eyeing the mall, the lumberyard, the whole network of Arthur businesses, in the way that lenders eye collateral that is more attractive than their money. If Stella had understood the precarious juncture George's speculations had reached, would they have done what they did at Lake Owatonna? If she ever suspected that he had known and nonetheless helped her do away with George, why...

Why, she might have emptied the safe-deposit box of its three quarters of a million dollars and let him think it was George who removed it.

Roy didn't believe this for a minute. He did not want to believe it. To believe it required him to think that his childhood sweetheart no longer loved him. But, taken simply as a logical possibility, the thought undeniably made sense. For Stella. Just as it would make sense for her to deny she knew anything about what Roy Hunt intended to do last February when the three of them went ice fishing on Lake Owatonna. There seemed no comparable logical possibility that enabled him to accuse Stella and himself escape the consequences of what they had done. That did not seem fair. Thank God he trusted Stella.

The seventh hole was a par five, the fairway bordered on the left by woods and on the right by a creek that joined the three ponds of the course. As he addressed his ball on the tee, Roy was far more conscious of the water hazard on the right than of the out-of-bounds and woods on his left. Thus, as so many had before him and many more would after, he dragged the ball to the left in a great banana-shaped curve that took it well into the woods.

His healthy curses split the evening air. He thought of hitting another but decided against it. He had already lost five balls. He did not intend to abandon the one he had hooked into the woods, let alone take the risk of losing another. He got into his cart and sped off to the edge of the fairway, where he parked and plunged into the woods in search of his ball.

It was his first time in these woods. In competition he always hit a safe iron from the seventh tee, and when he did use a wooden club, it was a slice not a hook that plagued him. So it was with some surprise that he learned the woods were not deep. Indeed, there was a steel structure at their far edge, a building he had first thought belonged to the country club. Curious, he walked along just inside the woods, studying the building, and then he saw that beyond it was a house and a swimming pool. A man stood beside the pool; his bald head and beard somehow lent him dignity, authority.

Seated in a chair a few feet from him and listening with rapt interest was Stella.

TEN

BEATRICE DEAN was Mr. Arthur's administrative assistant when he disappeared, and prior to that she had been his secretary. Only the title changed, her job had been pretty much the same ever since she came from Minneapolis to work for Rosemary's uncle eight years ago. She had given him her loyalty and served him as subjects once served monarchs. His success was hers. Almost from the beginning, she had no life outside her job. She had come to Fairland with the quite deliberate purpose of protecting him from the consequences of his wife's infidelity.

On fall and spring evenings, sitting on the deck of her house high above the river, watching what the setting sun did to the landscape and the water's surface, Beatrice would muse on how her life had turned on a mere accident. Accidents, really, and the first had been getting to know Rosemary.

They lived in the same building on Harmon Place, ugly on the outside, but the interior had been completely redone. Beatrice had a magnificent view of Loring Park from her living room window. She loved having views. All she needed for relaxation was to come home, relax, and take in the view. In Minneapolis it had been Loring Park, in Fairland it was the Father of Waters.

One evening in the lobby of the building, checking her mailbox, Beatrice pulled out an invitation from the bachelors on the first floor asking her to come to a party that Saturday night.

"A bachelor party?" said a girl who had come in just after Beatrice and also opened her mailbox. "That is an invitation you're reading, isn't it?"

Neither of them knew the bachelors. In any case, Beatrice was certain they were younger than her and, likely as not, younger than the other woman as well. Young or old, they would be shorter than Beatrice. The door of the first-floor apartment opened and a redheaded young man who seemed to have a congenital blush looked out.

"We're counting on you. I'm Fred."

There was a Fred among the four names at the bottom of the invitation.

"Why not?" the other girl said. She looked at Beatrice. "Okay?"

That is how she met Rosemary Burnet. They went to the party and it was very young and very drunk, but when it got too wild they adjourned to Beatrice's apartment and had the first of the long talks that were to form the heart of their friendship. It helped that they were both reconciled to being single. Rosemary had had a tragic love and could not even imagine herself loving another man. Beatrice's tragedy, if that's what it was, was the result of her height. She was five feet eleven inches tall. Thick brown hair, a heart-shaped face, an ample but shapely body—there was simply too much of her, physically, for the vast majority of the men she had so far met, and she was cursed with brains besides. All her relatives, all her friends, had been certain there was a perfect man for her somewhere, and perhaps there was. The first time she visited Fairland with Rosemary and met her Uncle George, Beatrice told herself that if she ever found a man like him her destiny would be fulfilled. But of course, in meeting George she had already met the man for her.

When she lived in Minneapolis, Beatrice worked out in the health center of the Hiawatha Hotel three afternoons a week. The first time she saw Rosemary's Aunt Stella in the hotel, she had been about to say hello when she saw that Mrs. Arthur was with someone, so she let it go. The second time, Stella was with the same man and Beatrice was not at all inclined to make herself known. She wondered if Stella even remembered the amazon her niece had brought down from Minneapolis the previous summer. Beatrice knew already that something was wrong.

Of course she said nothing to Rosemary. But it wasn't of Rosemary she thought immediately anyway. Having met the godlike George Arthur, Beatrice found it an unintelligible sacrilege that his wife, mere mortal Stella, should be doing whatever she was doing in Minneapolis with the little wimp she was always with. Disbelief, anger, then sadness were what she felt.

Of course, it might be perfectly innocent, she told herself. But she could not leave it alone. On the building directory where she worked there was listed DONOVAN ASS'S, an entry bound to catch the eye. Marvin the elevator operator saw nothing wrong when she pointed to it.

"He's a private eye," he said.

"What are the other asses?"

Marvin wore a hat worthy of a general. He did not turn around but continued to stare at the closed door as they rose in the elevator. Beatrice felt rebuffed, but in truth Marvin was hard-of-hearing. As if to prove that everything has a meaning, she recalled Donovan Ass's when she told herself she had to know for certain what Stella was up to.

It turned out that there were no associates, only Donovan, a middle-sized man in a gray suit and a plaid vest who seemed to be suppressing his eagerness when she asked about his fees. They depended. She thought what she wanted done was a simple matter. Donovan laid an index finger aside his nose and let his eyelids droop. Portrait of a man well acquainted with the surprising complexity of things. In the end, the inquiry cost her four hundred and eighty dollars. The results were unequivocal. Stella had a rendezvous with Roy Hunt, a Fairland banker and childhood friend, at least twice a month.

A week after Beatrice had acquired proof of Stella's infidelity, Rosemary mentioned that her uncle was coming to Minneapolis on business and would also be interviewing possible secretaries.

"Where?"

"Where what?"

"What employment agency is he using?"

"Are *you* interested?"

Beatrice managed to hesitate, and when she spoke her voice sounded blasé. "Should I be?"

"Beatrice, you've seen Fairland."

"I liked it."

"Why don't we call up my uncle and set up an appointment?"

"Would you?"

Rosemary hesitated, unable to believe that Beatrice was truly interested in moving to Fairland, Minnesota, when she was doing so well in Minneapolis.

Rosemary called. George Arthur did not remember meeting Beatrice, but he had a counterproposal. Why didn't the girl come to Fairland before the Minneapolis trip?

Two days later, Beatrice was seated across the desk from George Arthur. There were flecks of gray in his hair, the corners of his eyes wrinkled nicely when he thought or when the smile came and went on his wide manly mouth. It was the first time she had been able to study his face and she realized her memories had been inadequate. He was clearly impressed by her vita, the interview had gone very well, but he was puzzled.

"Fairland is not like Minneapolis."

"Are you a native?"

"No!"

"I suppose people wondered why you came."

He smiled. "I've done very well here."

She looked across the desk, saying nothing. He nodded.

"Okay. Let's talk salary."

That had been eight years ago. It now took an effort of will for Beatrice to remember her life in Minneapolis. She rented for a year and then bought and remodeled a silo high above the Mississippi. The silo looked more like a lighthouse now, its upper floor wrapped around with windows so that she had her choice of any point on the compass in which to look. Halfway up, on the river side, a kind of widow's walk had been built out over the bluff. Her bedroom was on the second highest level, a semicircular room with a circular bed. Fantasies she would not let form into distinct images plagued her when she bought and furnished her odd house. That it might be the love nest in which she would compensate for Stella's infidelity was an idea that shocked her not because of its lack of logic—how could his infidelity balance his wife's?—but for its presumption. Morality had nothing to do with it. George Arthur was her destiny, her fate. When he got to his feet and, looking down at her, shook her hand, signifying she was hired, the gesture was in its way as binding as a religious ceremony.

But the religion she entered made her a vestal virgin. If George Arthur saw her as a woman during her first half-dozen years in his employ, Beatrice was unaware of it. She swam every morning at the Y, she had an exercise room at home, she dressed in a muted but striking way; lesser men seemed aware of her charms, but to George Arthur she was a godsend of efficiency, the sexless machine that brought order to his business life. She might have been his slave. The truth was that this did not repel her. She *was* his slave. She belonged to him. It sufficed that she could live her life in his presence, working for him.

She would, of course, oh so willingly have accepted more. Stella's stolen lovemaking continued. Knowing what she knew, Beatrice was surprised that no one else noticed, but no one did, least of all George. It angered her that he should be duped by his wife, she longed to make it up to him, but she knew it would be fatal if she were the one to bring Stella's long-term affair to his attention. Sometimes she wished that Rosemary would discover her aunt's infidelity and blow the whistle.

"I can almost imagine living here myself," Rosemary said one Saturday afternoon, supine in a deck chair above the river, a glass of iced tea in her hand.

"You could live here," Beatrice said.

Rosemary tipped back the huge straw hat she wore as protection from the sun. "I'd never get any work done if I lived in Fairland. I associate it with adolescent indolence."

"It's like anywhere else," Beatrice lied.

"How's the job?"

"I like it."

"Uncle George sings your praises."

"He can't sing."

Beatrice decided that she did not want Rosemary to know about her aunt. The worst thing about what Stella was doing was that it made George look bad, somehow at fault. How could he not know what was going on? His ignorance suggested that he was not close to his wife. Beatrice came to imagine that she and George both led celibate lives, victims of star-crossed passion, doomed never to consummate their love but no less in love for that.

One morning he came in, stopped at her desk, leaned over, and kissed her on the cheek.

"Your sixth anniversary. We're going to lunch."

They crossed to the Wisconsin side of the river and from the dining room of the Belvedere Hotel Beatrice's converted silo was visible. She pointed it out.

"You live there!"

It hurt that he had never even wondered where she lived. Perhaps he thought she was still in the apartment she had rented her first year in Fairland. He was fascinated by her description of her dwelling.

"Come have a look."

They drove there from lunch, and George climbed the spiral staircases, stood in the upper room, and looked east and west and north and south, shaking his head with wonder.

"This is undoubtedly the best house in Fairland."

"It's not for sale."

She had read his mood correctly. She knew his manner when the acquisitive spirit was on him. His impulse was to want to own what he liked. So it was that her converted silo was the catalyst that brought her life in Fairland to fruition.

He started to stop by on weekends. He became a frequent presence on her deck, sipping a mild bourbon and water. He had peeked into her bedroom the first time and withdrawn his head without comment. Seated together on the deck, their conversation was a continuation of the business of the week. This oblique foreplay went on for months, but Beatrice was patient. She felt now that everything was foreordained. It was beyond anything she or he might will. It would happen. It did. One Sunday afternoon in winter.

He had stopped by to watch the Vikings game on her television. He did not need to tell her Stella was in Minneapolis.

"I'm surprised your television screen isn't circular."

"What do you mean?"

"There are no angles in your house, everything is round. Even your bed."

That he should remember and mention that almost surprised her. Snow beat against the Thermopane windows, the game was boring, his drink was stronger than usual. When she handed him a refill, she did not immediately let go of the glass. Their eyes met, he tugged her and the glass downward and for the first time their lips met.

That it was the first time, not a freak, seemed to be something they both knew. On the circular bed he was boyishly eager and it was far from perfect, but it didn't matter, they had the rest of their lives.

To his credit he felt guilty afterward. It was all she could do not to tell him he had nothing to feel bad about, he had been a victim for years. None of that mattered now. She wanted him to take their love seriously enough to feel bad that it was secret and stolen. And infrequent.

Stella might meet her Roy twice a month, but for Beatrice and George it was always an event, usually unplanned, at least overtly, and this prolonged their sense of being overwhelmed by something rather than causing it to come about by careful planning.

Once George became her lover, Beatrice felt less comfortable with Rosemary. Not that they saw one another much. The trouble was, they had so little in common other than Stella and George and that was a dangerous topic now. But apart from three days in Acapulco, Beatrice's affair with George consisted of the odd weekend afternoon in her circular bed.

Eventually, this was not enough for either of them. When George made his proposal that they simply go, disappear, Beatrice accepted without hesitation. Whatever he wanted to do she would do. Thank God she had not told him about Stella; his suggestion was made out of love for her untainted by knowledge of his wife's infidelity.

The last time they were together was when Stella went to Minneapolis on a weekday afternoon. Beatrice set the office phone to forward calls to her home. George had fallen asleep beside her when the phone rang and a woman asked to speak with Mr. Arthur.

"May I say who's calling?"

George had wakened and was now propped on his elbow, listening.

"This is his wife," the woman said.

It could not possibly be Stella's voice but the reference to Stella startled Beatrice. She forgot that the caller had rung the office and that the call had been automatically routed to her home phone. It was as if they had been discovered.

"One moment, please."

She handed the phone to George, shrugging. The sheet she had drawn against her fell away and George's eyes followed its descent. He swallowed before speaking into the phone.

"George Arthur speaking. Who is this?"

She watched the frown form. He took the phone from his ear, looked at it, handed it back to her. Beatrice had managed to cover herself again. She hung up the phone, waiting for George to speak.

"They hung up."

"It was a woman. She said it was your wife."

"Stella!"

"It wasn't her voice."

"Are you sure?"

"Positive."

"But who..."

She remembered now and reminded him of the telephone rerouting. The call had been made to the office. But neither of them knew what it meant. Nor did they have the time to discuss the matter. Fifteen minutes later they were at their desks downtown, trying to work, plagued by the mysterious phone call. There seemed little doubt that the woman who called knew about them and meant to frighten them. She had succeeded.

Later it seemed to Beatrice that she had known then that the end was in sight, but of course that was an illusion. By unspoken agreement, George stayed away from her place. How stupidly easy it would have been for someone to notice his visits there. He put his car beside hers in the double garage and closed the door, but his arrival and departure might be observed. This is what must have happened. Beatrice feared it meant the end.

But her fear had borne on the end of their affair, not the end of George's life.

When he was reported missing, Beatrice felt a cold hand grip her heart. It was no later reconstruction that from the beginning she knew he was dead. What nonsense to think he had stepped out of that fishing shack and just walked away. He had drowned as Roy Hunt said.

Roy Hunt.

Stella's lover.

George had told her he was going ice fishing with Roy, and Beatrice had been severely tempted to tell George the man was Stella's lover. If nothing else, she was stopped by the moral indignation the thought still brought. What right did she have to condemn Stella and Roy? If anything, she was grateful to them. So George had gone off with Roy Hunt, and with Stella too, it would turn out, to go ice fishing.

Reading the newspaper account of Roy's statement that George must have slipped through the hole chopped in the ice and drowned, and then the unbelievable skepticism of the local reporter and, apparently, the sheriff as well, Beatrice formed the certitude that Roy was responsible for George's death. Not just because he had invited him ice fishing that stormy day. Because he had killed him.

Eventually the details became clear: Stella had gone to the cabin while the two men fished. It had been a conspiracy, Beatrice assured herself. Roy and Stella had decided to kill George.

Why?

How could she not think it was out of knowledge of his affair with her? The betrayed wife's fury. But it was that same wife's lover who had been at the scene of George's death. Gradually Beatrice came to think that Stella had not known of her and George, that she and Roy had killed George in order that they might marry. And of course to come into possession of George's wealth.

During the three months before George was found, expecting nothing but what eventually occurred—his drowned body revealed by the melting sun of spring—Beatrice did what she and George had planned to do, transferring to her freezer chest the cash he had realized from the series of loans he had taken on the basis of the company's assets. When Beatrice put the meat back into the freezer she was covering three and a half million dollars with T-bones, pork chops, ribs, and packages of ground beef.

At George's funeral, she had not wept. Her grief was months old by then and she had learned to see her life as the meticulous carrying out of the plans she and George had made. Rosemary was at the funeral, of course, and it brought the old friends together again, particularly when Stella asked Rosemary to redecorate the house.

"Did you ever see George's library?"

"No."

"Weren't you ever in that house?"

"I was his secretary, Rosemary, not a social friend."

"Fairland isn't big enough to accommodate such distinctions."

"What about the library?"

Stella was selling off in what Rosemary clearly regarded unseemly haste the collection of which George was so proud. Of course Beatrice knew of his love for books. He had often shaken his head with disapproval at the mysteries and thrillers she read, but he had felt no compulsion to convert her to more demanding fare.

"It's as if she wants to erase every memory of him from the house."

Beatrice could not share Rosemary's disapproval. As far as Beatrice was concerned, the essential George had nothing to do with Stella or the house he had shared with her. Besides, Beatrice knew how little Stella stood to profit from her husband's death, and if, as Beatrice believed, Stella had murdered George, her punishment would be sweet to behold.

When she arranged to have dinner with Rosemary at the country club it was in the hope she would be brought up to date on Stella. Beatrice continued at her desk at Arthur Enterprises and knew that those who had loaned money to the dead president were curious about the collateral that secured those loans. Arthur Enterprises continued to thrive, but Beatrice knew that this prosperity now belonged to the banks, not to Stella.

"What are you drinking?" Rosemary asked, eyeing Beatrice closely when she joined her in the country club dining room.

"Do you want something?"

"You're not drinking?"

Beatrice laughed. Her jaw was still numb from the novocaine the dentist had given her that afternoon. Rosemary seemed relieved by the explanation.

"I tell you, everyone else is becoming unglued so why not you?"

"Who's everyone else?"

"Stella told me to stop work on the house."

"Why?"

"Is it possible she's strapped for money?"

"I don't see how. Business is booming."

An unwise remark. There was no way she could claim not to know about the loans George had taken out. Fortunately, Rosemary was distracted.

"Oh my God. Here comes Roy Hunt."

ELEVEN

STELLA FOUND the bookstore airless and stifling and asked if they couldn't talk outside.

"Is there any point in talking further, Mrs. Arthur?"

"Oh, I haven't come to the purpose of my visit yet."

The conversation to this point had turned on her alleged desire to buy back the books she had sold him. He insisted that he could not let them go for less than five thousand dollars. Stella was certain she could have gotten a lower price if she really wanted the books but she didn't. She was here because Roy had told her of Nicodemus's visit to the bank and admission to the safe-deposit boxes.

"We can sit by the pool," he said, his expression a mixture of pique and curiosity.

"Perfect. Maybe I'll fall in."

She was walking toward the door when she said that. Was it her imagination that her silly remark reminded him too of George's death? His gaze seemed palpable on her back. The damnable door jingled when she pushed it open. Stella wanted to stop and inhale lungfuls of fresh air. Nicodemus closed the door, went around her, and led the way to the pool, where she sat in a deck chair and refused his offer of a drink.

"Sure? I'm going to get a beer."

"I'm sure."

How slowly he moved, shuffling up the narrow walk that joined the house to the pool. Annoyance gave way to envy. What a peaceful life Nicodemus had contrived for himself. To Stella the bookseller's life seemed without worry or trouble, an endless undemanding duration spent in a genteel world. It seemed less a business than a hobby. But he had been hard-nosed as hell about George's books. Stella looked away from the house toward the woods. Beyond was the country club where she would meet Roy later. What if Nicodemus agreed to sell the books back to her? Could she afford to buy them? The question made her shiver despite the afternoon sun that slanted through the trees and warmed her. At the moment, she did not want to spend any money at all. She had asked Rosemary to stop redecorating the house. The empty safe-deposit box had been bad enough, but now Roy suggested that George's death would leave her in the same predicament her father's had.

"Stella, he owes me six hundred thousand. We collected interest during the months of waiting. It's been six weeks since interest has been paid. Technically, I could foreclose..."

"I will kill you if you do." She had not raised her voice; there was no anger in her tone. But he knew she meant it.

"Of course I won't. But there are others."

"I'll pay the interest."

"Better check with Beatrice."

"Beatrice! What does she have to do with it?"

"She's been acting as president since George's disappearance. She always took over when George traveled."

"Did she?"

"Someone had to. It was an arrangement with George."

"I see."

"No you don't. You don't want to see. The whole damned thing could collapse, Stella."

What the consequences of that would be was written on his face. Would Roy still love her if for the second time she was robbed of a fortune? His gloomy report on the condition of the business made the money missing from the safe-deposit box all the more important. What had Nicodemus been doing at the bank, in the vault where the safe-deposit boxes were?

"He has a box."

"How convenient."

Roy said nothing, only made a face. What did she mean by the remark? That Nicodemus had transferred the contents of George's box to his own?

"Look and see," she urged Roy.

"Look and see? And how am I supposed to do that?"

"Surely you must have a key."

"It takes two, Stella, as you damned well know."

"You don't have a copy of the customer's?"

"What would be the point of two keys if I could open a box?"

"But what if someone dies?"

She stopped him after several minutes. She really did not want to hear about the procedure for opening the box of a deceased person whose key could not be found. She had a sudden intuition of what had happened.

Rosemary's remark about money hidden in a book suggested where George's copy of the key to the unlisted safe-deposit box had been. It was a flat key and

would easily lie between the pages of a book. Nicodemus had found the key, had gotten into the box and
transferred all that cash to his own box.

When she told Roy this, he shook his head, smiling
sadly.

"He couldn't get in. He can't claim to be a dead
man."

"Or sign George's name?"

"Or sign George's name."

"But George's name is not registered, is it?"

"No, it isn't. Which makes it doubly impossible.
Any such effort would come immediately to my attention."

But that only revived her doubts about Roy. In any
case, she meant to visit Nicodemus and see if she could
in any way prove or disprove her theory. She was
counting on further inspiration.

But it was luck rather than inspiration that made her
visit a success. While they talked in the bookstore,
Nicodemus pulled open the drawer of his desk in
search of matches and Stella's eye alighted on a small
red envelope. He did not close the drawer tightly
again. It was all she could do not to cry out. Was it his
or hers? After luck, inspiration came to her aid.

"Is that an Edna St. Vincent Millay I see?"

She was pointing to a shelf above his head. He
turned slowly, looked up, and nodded.

"*Fatal Interview*. A first edition."

"Could I see it?"

"You like her poetry?"

"Once I could recite whole sonnets by heart."

He pushed back from the desk, rose to his feet, and
pulled a rolling ladder into place. Before he had
mounted two rungs, she had slipped the envelope from

the desk drawer and into her purse. Flushed with success, she almost bought the Millay volume, but the price he quoted cleared her mind.

"Honestly, I think I may enter the book business myself."

"Your husband could have. He had more books than I did when I started."

That was when she complained of the stuffiness of the store and suggested they go outside. If the key she now had was Nicodemus's, she and Roy could check the contents of his box. Best not to think of that. Thought of distinctly, the idea was crazy, but she could force Roy to do it.

"I love this time of day," Nicodemus said beside her. Stella was almost startled. How silently he had returned. The can of beer looked diminutive in his paw of a hand. He eased himself with sighs and groaning into a chair like hers. "Now what was the purpose of your visit?"

"When will you unpack my husband's books?"

"I won't if you intend to..."

"No. You bought them, they're yours. But I would like to be here when you take them out of the boxes."

"Your niece expressed the same desire."

"Did she?"

"Are you missing something?"

Had his voice altered when he asked the question? She let the silence build. His eyes drifted away toward the woods.

"Do people leave things in books?"

"All the time. It's one of the bonuses of buying them."

"That's why I'd like to help you unpack George's books."

"I wish you'd thought of this at the house."

"So do I. Have you opened any of them?"

"Is there something in particular you want to look for?"

"A key."

He almost jumped. "What kind of a key?"

"To the grandfather clock."

Despite the beard, his reactions were unmistakable. The mention of a key had filled him with confusion; specifying it was a clock key made him sag with relief. It was tempting to just flat out ask him if he had a safe-deposit box, but she decided against that. He would go check his desk and know who had taken the red envelope. She rose to her feet.

"I suppose a jeweler could get another key for the clock, but it would be simpler if I found the old one."

Nicodemus stood too, as if anxious to get her on her way.

"Thank you for your patience, Mr. Nicodemus."

He nodded. His beer can, she noticed, was almost crushed in his grip. He started to accompany her to her car, but she stopped that. Having turned her car around on the gravelly drive, she headed out to the county road. As she neared it, a car full of kids screamed past, going well over seventy, the pulsing blast of rock music trailing in its wake. It made Stella alert and when she entered the road, although no car was coming in either direction, she took off with a squealing of tires and the spit of gravel on her fenders.

The hospital stood where the road became a city street. Stella pulled into the parking lot, opened her purse, and took out the little red envelope. The flat key was inside it. Now Roy had no excuse. If this was Nicodemus's key, they would open his box.

Her mind turned to Beatrice. She had never liked tall women and she particularly did not like Beatrice with her doglike devotion to George. George of course loved it. He would have liked all women to defer to him the way Beatrice did. Beatrice had treated her as an intruder whenever she stopped by George's office, and been overtly insolent. Stella blotted out the memory of the humiliation she had suffered.

Beatrice acting as president.

Beatrice failing to pay interest on loans which, if they were called in, would bring down Arthur Enterprises. Who did the woman think she was? Her title was administrative assistant and there was no longer an administrator for her to assist. Well, Beatrice Dean would have to go. Stella looked at her watch. Ye gods, she was late for dinner with Roy.

Stella put the car in gear, eased out of her parking space, and drove across the lot, on her way to the country club.

At the club she dawdled in the powder room despite the fact that she was already half an hour late. Roy was no doubt comfortable in the bar or already at table, having his drink. She leaned toward her mirrored self and tried to surprise in her eyes her feelings for Roy. That he might be inconvenienced by her tardiness did not cause her pain. If anything she enjoyed it, it was a way of punishing him, but for what? Because she blamed him for the empty safe-deposit box for one thing. She blamed him because everything seemed to be going wrong. Damn the Poeglins! Fear of what they might say about seeing her with Roy in a Minneapolis hotel had led to Lake Owatonna. How could they have harmed her? And of course there had been another solution to the problem. Stop seeing Roy, call it quits, stop this silly meeting here and there. She might have made up her mind to love her own husband.

The image of George rose in her mind, eclipsing Roy, reminding Stella of her father, and she had the sick feeling that she had done a very stupid thing and was going to have to pay for it.

The only way she could quash the memory of George was by concentrating on her lips, applying rouge, not looking herself in the eye.

The bar was all but empty. Those who weren't in the dining room were having drinks on the veranda. Roy was not on the veranda.

Windows from the veranda looked into the dining room and it was through one of them that Stella caught a glimpse of Roy at a table with two women. Rosemary and Beatrice. Beatrice!

Stella stepped back from the window and took a wicker chair on the veranda from which she could look unobtrusively at Roy and her niece and Beatrice. She caught the eye of a waiter and ordered a whiskey sour. Roy's remarks drummed in her head. Beatrice was sitting in for George. Beatrice had not paid the interest on the loans. Beatrice.

Her drink came and she took a very long swallow. Suddenly she felt surrounded by hostile forces. The thought she did not like to think refused to be dismissed. I conspired to murder my husband. She could imagine the headlines, the story of the trial, the snickers and nods and condemnations, particularly by other women. Spoiled daughter, pampered wife, unfaithful spouse. Oh, she could write the stories herself, who better? Photographs of the love nests that had been identified. What a series that would make. If she were to read such a story, Stella knew what she would feel for the wife and her lover.

Lover. Roy Hunt. The question would arise why she had risked everything for Roy Hunt. By comparison George was as Hyperion to a satyr. She would be seen as one who flung away her inheritance for a mess of pottage. The ultimate irony would be for Roy to turn on her, betray her, leave her.

Stella held her empty glass to her lips. Roy had killed George. Perhaps that could never be proved, but if it could, would her complicity be clear? Stella thought about it for fifteen minutes and was convinced that the only thing linking her with what happened to George was Roy's word. Of course he would say he did it for her.

As an insurance policy she must make certain that, should he ever say she was involved, his accusation would be dismissed. She looked through the window at the dining room. Rosemary was not at the table and Roy was leaning forward speaking to an obviously interested Beatrice as if they had been waiting for Rosemary to give them this chance.

What would Beatrice say if she knew she was speaking to George's murderer?

TWELVE

"WELL, SHE'S certainly in a hurry," Mabel said beside Babs as they neared the Nicodemus driveway and a car with a woman at the wheel roared into the road and went barreling toward town.

"I think that was Stella Arthur," Babs said. "What on earth would she be doing here?"

"Bothering poor Steve." Mabel sighed. "Honestly, I wish we hadn't bought those books. She can't make up her mind whether she really wants to let them go."

Babs wanted to hear more about that, so when Mabel asked her to stay for supper she agreed. She called Louis at his office to suggest he get a bite at the club, but she got only the answering machine. She told it what she would have told Louis and dialed home. No answer. Well, he always checked the answering machine. Louis had them both on the latest diet that had caught his attention and the promise of grilled hamburgers would have undone Babs even if she weren't dying to hear more about Stella Arthur pestering Steve Nicodemus.

"Take this out, would you?" Mabel said, handing her the salad.

Babs pushed the screen door open with her hip and went down the narrow walk to the pool apron on which Steve was setting up his grill.

"Mabel asked me to stay," Babs said when Steve turned from the grill. She tried to sound sultry but the words came out slightly strangled.

For years Babs had struggled to be a good wife, a good Unitarian—or rather, as she would have put it, struggled and succeeded. How silly it seemed now to speak of the life she led as the result of a struggle. Ever since she had put two and two together where Stella and Roy Hunt were concerned, and discovered more envy than condemnation in her heart, Babs had been inviting temptation. To no avail. Compared to her previous condition she had indeed been struggling, but she had not had so much as a nibble at second remove. Talking with Mabel about such things wasn't much help.

"Half of modern fiction is based on illicit love," Mabel said authoritatively. "At least it used to be. With the collapse of the moral code, breaches of it lose their dramatic interest. Hence the decline in fiction."

Was fiction declining? Mabel was a librarian and ought to know, but how then could Steve make a living buying and selling books?

"They're collectibles for most of our clients. Objects to possess, not books to be read."

It was not always easy to keep Mabel on the topic, but of course Mabel didn't know what the topic was. Babs could hardly come right out and ask her new friend if she had every been untrue to her husband. Mabel had such a matronly air, it was almost sacrilegious to think of her stepping out on Steve. The reverse seemed less unlikely, men being what they are.

If Steve ever saw her as a woman, however, Babs was unaware of it. In his eyes, she was just a friend of Mabel's. But then again, what had she thought of

him, a bald man with a beard and a belly, preoccupied, smoking a pipe, his conversation largely a matter of humming, grunts, gestures. But when he turned
from the grill he was a man Stella Arthur had been
bothering, and Babs knew all about Stella.

"Stella nearly ran us down when she drove out of
here."

"Strange woman."

"Oh?"

He looked at her over his glasses. "Is she a friend of
yours?"

"If she's a friend of yours."

He didn't know what to make of that, but then Babs
had surprised herself. How daring it sounded. The
universe seemed to be going on as before, however,
and she was emboldened.

"Is she making a pest of herself?"

He sighed.

"The merry widow," Babs said. "But then she was
a merry wife before that."

"Of Windsor?"

Mabel joined them, bearing a tray laden with buns
and mustard and ketchup and napkins and silver-
ware. She put it down on the picnic table.

"Who's a merry wife?"

"We were discussing Stella," Babs said, giving Steve
a conspiratorial glance.

"Please," Mabel cried. "Not while I'm eating.
How's the meat doing?"

Mabel and Babs ate at the table, but Steve drew a
small table next to a deck chair and ate there.

"What did Stella want?" Mabel asked.

Her husband put up a hand to indicate he was
chewing. They waited until he swallowed.

"I don't think she herself knows. First, she talked about buying the books back, but she doesn't want to pay any more for them than we gave her. I explained every way I can that it doesn't work that way. Then she indicated why she wants them."

"Why?"

"She can't find a key."

"A key! What kind of key?"

"She said a clock key."

"She said? Don't you believe her?"

"Do you?"

Mabel thought about it. "It depends on the clock," she said, and burst out laughing.

"It's just an excuse," Babs said.

"An excuse for what?"

"What you said. To bother Steve."

Once more Mabel burst out laughing. Babs's eyes met Steve's and she was surprised to see fear in his. Fear of what? He certainly couldn't be afraid of her. Babs smiled, picking up the merriment of Mabel's laughter, wanting to reassure Steve, but he pushed his chair back and stood.

"Anyone else want a beer?"

"I'd love a beer," Babs trilled.

She had three beers before she went, two more than she wanted, one more than Mabel really wanted her to have. Babs was conscious of her friend's wondering how long she would stay. Had she assumed Babs would turn down the invitation to eat? No doubt. She did not want Mabel thinking of her what she had said of Stella, that she was bothering Steve.

In any case, she wasn't. Steve spent most of the time not looking at her. He had brought out the evening paper and used that as a shield against the women's conversation, but each time he went inside and asked as a formality if she wanted another beer, Babs said yes, if only to get his attention. She felt like a schoolgirl desperately trying to interest a boy.

She didn't finish her third beer and she spent the last fifteen minutes of her visit talking directly to Mabel, not intending to be overheard by Steve, girl talk.

"When are we going to take a trip to Minneapolis?"

"Steve is going next week."

Babs ignored this now, being a good girl. "I mean us."

"What could we do in Minneapolis we can't do here?"

"You could help me at the Erickson auction," Steve said from behind his newspaper.

Mabel shook her head and made a face at Babs.

"The Erickson auction," Babs repeated.

Mabel told her about the estate sale that would take place the following week in Minneapolis, everything in the stately Erickson home that looked out on Lake of the Isles. Her account was supplemented by remarks from Steve. Erickson, it seemed, had prospered in milling and acquired a large library; his wife had furnished their home with antiques. Steve would go up the day before to examine the library in anticipation of the bidding on Wednesday.

Mabel and Steve were still on it when Babs left.

Driving slowly home in the dusk, she smiled vaguely as she thought of going to Minneapolis on Tuesday and just running into Steve at the Erickson mansion near Lake of the Isles. A daydream, of course. She exorcised it by kidding herself that if she went she would probably run into Stella too. Stella.

When George Arthur disappeared so soon after Babs and Louis had run into Stella and Roy Hunt in Minneapolis, it was difficult not to see a connection between the two events, particularly since Roy had been with George when he disappeared.

"Not even to me, Barbara," Louis said with cold fury when she tried to talk with him about it. "Never so much as hint at such a thing again."

"You think it's all coincidence?"

"I think that neither of us should think about it. This is a small town. Such gossip could ruin a person's life."

"Gossip!"

"What would you call it?"

She was so angry she couldn't talk. She didn't talk to Louis for four and a half days, but the silence punished her more than it apparently did him. Her karate class, something Claudia had talked her into, proved a welcome safety valve. What angered her most was that Louis was right. What else was the story about Stella and Roy but gossip?

During the months before the body was found, Babs felt they were waiting for some great revelation, but the body was found, weeks passed, and there seemed to be no questioning of the preliminary finding that George Arthur had died in an ice-fishing accident. There was a warning look in Louis's eye when the subject came up and Babs never alluded to the episode in Minneapolis.

Stella ran around free and so did Roy Hunt and it looked as if they were going to get away with what increasingly Babs was certain they had done. George had been in their way so they had removed him. Imagine the town believing that a man like George Arthur could fall through a hole in the ice in a fishing shack. But then George was still regarded as a newcomer, no matter that he had married Stella and owned the largest business enterprise in Fairland.

Sometimes Babs imagined calling the sheriff anonymously, as she had called George Arthur's office when she and Louis returned from Minneapolis, and whispering that Stella and Roy Hunt had been carrying on for years and couldn't that be a motive. If Louis and the sheriff were not in the same lodge, she might have done it. But Louis would know immediately who had called the sheriff.

The house was dark when she turned into the drive and pressed the device that activated the garage door and switched on the outside lights. She wasn't surprised. Louis was unlikely to get home until late.

There was nothing on television worth watching so Babs took her paperback romance upstairs and read until her eyes would no longer stay open. It was eleven-thirty when she turned off the light.

She came awake with terror rising through her throat. Someone was shaking her violently. A hand was clamped over her mouth to stifle her scream. And then she made out Louis's face, distorted by the lamp beside her bed. Had he gone mad? He held his hand over her mouth until he was certain she would not scream again. She had never seen such an expression on his face before.

"You silly stupid woman," he said through clenched teeth. "You simply could not keep your mouth shut, could you?"

"Louis..."

"Sheriff Ewbank told me about the anonymous call he received about Stella and Roy. I told you never to mention that episode to anyone ever."

"I didn't!" she cried. "I didn't!"

The passion of her response made him hesitate, but he shook the denial away.

"Don't lie to me."

She pulled herself free of him, enraged that he should treat her like a child. Throwing back the covers, she got out of the bed on the opposite side and glared at her husband.

"I did not tell the sheriff or anyone else what we saw. Period. How dare you accuse me of such a thing."

That it was something she might have done, something she had wanted to do, faded before the simple truth that she had not done it. She spoke from the great strength of that fact, and her confidence in herself and contempt for Louis mounted as she repeated her denial.

"I don't understand," he said, genuinely confused.

"That is obvious enough. Are you drunk? Coming home and waking me like that. I might have had a heart attack."

"There is nothing wrong with your heart," he said wearily

"What is wrong with your head?"

"Someone called the sheriff and told him Stella had been having an affair with Roy Hunt."

"And you assumed it was me. Did you tell him that?"

"Good God, no."

"I'm surprised."

A wave of doubt swept over his face. "Are you lying to me, Babs?"

She snatched up the phone and threw it across the bed at him. The receiver bounced off the wall and an electric buzz filled the air.

"Call the goddamn sheriff and tell him I was the one who phoned. You don't believe me. Let's let everyone in on it."

Undeniably it was heady to be so completely in the right. There followed the silent treatment. After four and a half days he apologized, over the phone, calling from the office.

"It seemed the only explanation," he said.

"No doubt others found out what we did."

There was silence on the line, and she could just see him grinding his teeth.

She said, "I am going to Minneapolis to shop tomorrow."

"You'll have to go alone, Babs."

"I intend to."

Even as she profited from his mistake, she sensed that she would have to pay for her triumph eventually. Meanwhile, she would reap its advantages.

On Tuesday, driving to Minneapolis, to keep her mind off what she hoped might happen there, she wondered who might have called the sheriff. Who else knew that Stella and Roy had been playing around before George died?

THIRTEEN

RAIN FELL steadily and Steve Nicodemus welcomed it as a companion to his insomnia. He had left the bedroom and sat now in the breezeway enjoying the distraction of the storm. Each flash of lightning seemed an accusing finger pointed at him, each rumble of thunder signaled divine disapproval, but the rain itself was the promise of cleansing forgiveness.

Mrs. Arthur's unnerving visit had been all the proof he needed that even if the wealth of Croesus were within his grasp, he would be unable to take it. To steal it. Thus conscience doth make fair-to-middling non-evildoers of us all.

What would you do if no one knew what you were doing? The old undergraduate question. Plato's question too, the ring of Gyges rendering you invisible so that you might do what you would unobserved. Is it only the judgment of others that stops us from being worse than we are? In the past weeks, Steve felt that he had been subjected to a series of temptations, and he did not like what his reaction to them revealed about himself. He wished he had never heard of George Arthur's books.

The fact that they were still largely unpacked, still in the beer cases he and Mabel had transported them in, summed up how different this deal was. Not because it was local, although it was by far the largest library he had bought within a radius of fifty miles. In most instances, after the bid was accepted and the books brought to Fairland the seller was never heard from again, but now Steve felt that he had entered into some continuing relation with the Widow Arthur.

Widow. She was ten years and more younger than Mabel, a stranger to want, spoiled. It hurt that he had conferred moral superiority on that shallow woman by keeping the key he had found in one of her husband's books. He pressed his eyes closed but opened his heart to the sound of the steadily falling rain. On the stage of his eyelids the melodrama playing itself out, a silent movie in flickering black and white.

Honest bookdealer comes into possession of dead man's safe-deposit key. Surprise expressed by rounded eyes. He holds key in front of his face and other thoughts succeed surprise in exaggerated form. A shadow falls across the countenance. An evil thought has come. The key holds the promise of wealth. Greed contorts the actor's face. The key is returned to its envelope and clutched in his hand before he carefully hides it away on his person.

A moment of temptation was one thing, but to prolong it by keeping the key, even going to the bank in the mad hope that he would find a way to open Arthur's safe-deposit box! Had he really managed to check for Arthur's card in that file box? And now the key was hidden in his own box, his and Mabel's. He shook his head. He wished he could light his pipe, but that meant a trip inside and he did not want to move.

Mabel. The fact that he had not mentioned the key to her told the story. Her assumption would have been that the key was worthless, an old one somehow forgotten. Keeping it would have had no moral significance.

The problem with that was the obvious newness of the envelope. Or perhaps it had simply not been used often. It didn't matter. As soon as he thought of it as operative he should have returned it. There should have been no hesitation. What in the name of God had he been thinking?

The book business was a trade, he had done well at it, but it was far more than a business to Steve Nicodemus. He had arranged his whole life to bring about their present situation, served that long stretch in the Minneapolis Fire Department so they would always have the pension to fall back on, positioned himself to go into business when he did not need any dramatic success to make a go of it, chosen Fairland as his base of operations. It had been everything they dreamed. It was the best of both worlds. By keeping that key he jeopardized what had taken decades to build, and worse, he was treating unearned wealth, stolen wealth, as if it were the purpose of life.

And what about Rosemary? Talking with her, he had let all sorts of heated hopes and schemes form in his mind, he had permitted the beginning of lust to enter his heart. The elders who had attempted to seduce Susannah had been held up to ridicule for thousands of years, as hypocrites, yes, but prior to that as aging lechers. What is more comic and repellent than an old satyr in pursuit of a young woman? He could admit it to himself at three in the morning, sitting in the breezeway, surrounded by the sound of rain. He had lusted after the woman in his heart.

After all these years he had nearly succumbed to temptations ruinous of his business and of his marriage. When had these cracks in his character begun?

He deserved to be plagued by Stella Arthur. Of course, calling the key a clock key was teasing, a way of letting him know she had good reason to think he had found the key. Why hadn't she asked him straight out if he had found a safe-deposit key among her husband's books? He should have been protected by the fact that he had not yet unpacked the books, but his guilt would not allow him to make excuses. Once he started to deny or explain, she would know for certain he had the key. How had she first suspected him anyway? It was obvious enough to Steve that she thought he had it. He had been observed at the bank by Mr. Hunt.

He groaned aloud. He sat on the edge of a chair, hands crossed on his stomach, body bent forward, rocking slightly. Just because the woman in charge of the safe-deposit boxes was stupid didn't mean everyone in the bank was. He could have been seen rifling through those cards. He had been seen by Mr. Roy Hunt himself, president of the bank. Could Hunt open the Nicodemus box and find the missing key? The fact that Hunt had been with George Arthur when he drowned seemed to provide some logical glue to hold these thoughts together.

Alone in the night, sleepless in the breezeway of his secluded house, Steve Nicodemus felt himself the object of all eyes. That he had not actually done anything wrong was some consolation, but it could not diminish the impact of what all this told him about himself.

"Steve?"

It was Mabel. "I'm out here."

"Where?"

"On the breezeway."

"But it's raining."

When the wind gusted, a fine spray got to him from time to time, but he scarcely noticed. Mabel stood in the doorway.

"Is anything wrong?"

"No."

"There's milk of magnesia in the cupboard over the sink."

"I feel fine. I couldn't sleep."

A clink of chains as she lowered herself onto the swing. "The thunder woke me."

Lightning illumined the porch and outlined the lumpy form of his wife on the swing. Steve got up and sat beside her, putting an arm around her.

"What's wrong, Steve?"

"Not a thing," he said, almost jauntily. And there wouldn't be. In the morning, first thing, he would give that damned key to Mrs. Arthur and put the whole silly business behind him. Mabel pressed against him.

"It's nice out here."

"It is now." He squeezed her.

"Now you sound like Babs Poeglin."

"I do look a lot like her."

"She must be going through a phase."

"Oh?"

"She has the notion that everyone else is doing things she doesn't know about, that she's missing out on the fun."

"She reads too much."

"Or not enough. Most people would say she has a pretty full life."

"What does she want?"

Mabel laughed. "Adventure."

"Why doesn't she go on a cruise?"

"Her husband doesn't want to and anyway it's him she wants to get away from."

"Leave him?"

"No, no. I can't explain it."

"Do you mean she wants to play around?"

"When she asked if I'd like to go shopping in Minneapolis, she makes it sound like, well, I don't know what. It's awful saying these things about her. I like her."

She fell silent. The lightning and thunder stopped and there was only the sibilant sound of rain. Mabel pressed warmly against him and they rocked slightly in the swing.

"Wanna wrestle?"

"Steve."

"I don't mean out here."

A soft giggle. Her manner said yes. For a moment he thought of taking her in his arms and carrying her to their bed. But that would have made him useless if he got there. Not that Mabel was heavy. Well, she was no feather but he was bent out of shape himself. He stood and tugged her to her feet and, bumping hips, they went inside.

HIS COPY of their safe-deposit key was not in his desk drawer when he looked for it the following morning. He emptied the contents, piling things on the desktop, took the drawer out and looked underneath it. He searched the area around the desk, under the scrutiny of Zeno the cat. An early morning golfer made the back wall vibrate when his ball banged against it. Where was the key? He moved a book on his desk. The poems of Edna St. Vincent Millay. Ah. Zeno now sat where she had sat. Stella could have taken the key when he was getting the book. Tit for tat? Good God. Could she now open his box and find the missing key? If anything, his situation was more ambiguous than before.

He could scarcely go to Mrs. Arthur and accuse her of stealing the key.

The obvious course was one he did not dare take, namely to ask Mabel for her copy of their key, go to the bank, and open up the safe-deposit box and see if the key was still there. He was certain Hunt would be on watch to see him do that. A game of cat-and-mouse was in progress and he had become the mouse.

He realized that he was staring into Zeno's inscrutable gaze. Do cats think? What would Zeno do in his master's place?

He told himself that nothing could be done to harm him. If someone else opened their safe-deposit box without permission . . . Could legal permission be obtained? He felt that he had failed at failure, succumbed to temptation only to be rescued by the cunning of another, prevented from pursuing evil rather than turning it aside. And now he was more vulnerable than before.

"Do you really want me to go with you?" Mabel asked Monday night, her tone dutiful. She hated going to Minneapolis.

"No."

"One of these days we're going to have to unpack our new acquisitions. Want me to get started on the Arthur books?"

"There's no rush."

"I'll come with you."

"No." He added, as if it were important, "It's your day to work at the library."

"That's right."
Had she really forgotten?

THE FOLLOWING day, when he got to the Interstate and headed north, something like peace of mind came over him. He felt that he was escaping something malevolent. Ahead lay Minneapolis and the excitement of a legendary collection. He would be bidding against some of the biggest dealers in the Midwest but he was determined to buy some portion of the Erickson collection if it was everything it was said to be.

If his bid was successful, he would make certain when he packed the books that they contained no surprises. He did not want to come upon another key.

FOURTEEN

THE PRESENCE of the ineffable Roy Hunt had a sobering effect on Beatrice. Rosemary couldn't imagine anything duller than the banker's idea of small talk. He had just played nine holes and assumed they would like a blow-by-blow account.

"I'm just passing time until Stella gets here. We're dining together."

Beatrice looked at Rosemary and then let her eyes drift heavenward.

"Beatrice and I haven't had a good talk in ages. That's why I'm in town."

The hint fell on deaf ears. Roy nodded absentmindedly, as if considering what he would say next to amuse them. Beatrice's call urging her to come for a few days had Rosemary in a receptive mood. She had just completed two very satisfying jobs, a condominium and a lake home in Minnetonka. She had been toying with the idea of two weeks in the Loire Valley; she could fly into De Gaulle, rent a car, and just disappear.

"I certainly can't compete with that," Beatrice had said sadly.

"Oh I don't know. The Mississippi valley has its charms. What I want to do is vegetate."

"That's our specialty. We vegetate so well we consider vegetarianism akin to cannibalism. And you and I can talk."

That conjured up wonderful memories of Harmon Place and long evenings spent just talking. Beatrice knew about Russ and that made her very special to Rosemary. They had known one another a year when she divulged it. She still could not believe she had told Steve Nicodemus so easily. Thoughts of the book dealer decided her. She told Beatrice she would be glad to come visit.

"Fairland triumphs over France. I can't believe it. I am grateful, Rosemary."

"I want to enjoy the fruits of my labor."

Rosemary had worked closely with the architect who redesigned the silo. Beatrice's home was Rosemary's idea of an all but perfect dwelling. Of course it wouldn't have done for a family, but for a couple or a single person it was ideal. When she was rich she would retire, move in with Beatrice, and spend the rest of her life checking the points of the compass and watching Old Man River flow by below.

"If you go out after six you can play nine holes in an hour and fifteen minutes," Roy said. "That's with a cart, of course."

"Did Stella golf with you?"

He hesitated before answering. He smiled oddly. "I must ask her if she'd like to someday."

Rosemary excused herself and when she returned Roy Hunt finally left them. Beatrice said, "Did you notice the way he acted when you asked about Stella?"

"Stella told me they were childhood lovers."

"Who never grew up," Beatrice said, lifting her brows. "Turn around slowly and look out on the veranda."

Rosemary turned and saw nothing.

Beatrice said, "She's gone. Your aunt has been sitting out there for fifteen minutes watching this table."

"What on earth for?"

"How well do you know Stella?"

Rosemary shrugged. "As well as I want to, I guess."

The other diners were beginning to fall silent and look toward the entrance of the room where Stella and Roy were visible, their voices increasingly audible in the growing silence. Stella was practically screaming at Roy who, aware they were making a spectacle of themselves, glanced with horror at the fascinated audience. He took Stella's arm, but she shook herself free and stormed away. Roy, casting a stricken look toward the dining room, disappeared after her.

Rosemary looked at Beatrice. "Good Lord."

"A lovers' quarrel?"

"Do you suppose he was waiting for her here and she was waiting for him outside?"

"She knew he was here. We were under surveillance."

"I know Stella. She was waiting for him to come looking for her. And eventually he did. With results heard and seen by everyone. She had the exquisite pleasure of being stood up *and* getting the last word. Stella always gets the last word."

"I almost feel sorry for that awful man."

"They grew up together. Maybe they'll marry now."

"Now that the impediments have been removed?"

Rosemary did not pick up on these barbed remarks as she was sure Beatrice wanted her to. She did not want to encourage her old friend to assume the cliché role—secretary despises boss's wife.

The noise in the dining room never regained its previous level, doubtless because everyone was whispering about the scene Stella had just put on. The pianist whose dutiful playing had been ignored by the diners now became audible and Beatrice began to hum along.

"Cole Porter," she sighed.

An hour later, when they were at their ease in the windowed upper room, Beatrice put Cole Porter on her CD player and sang along. She had the elegant lyrics by heart, her voice was true, Rosemary lounged on a couch and, looking out, saw a falling star. It was a beautiful sight but it gave her a scary sense of the fragility of the universe. That star might have been many times the size of the earth.

During the night, a barrage of thunder and lightning wakened Rosemary, but it subsided into a steady rain to whose soothing liquid lullaby she spent several hours between sleep and waking, feeling a peace she had not felt in years.

Beatrice was up and gone before Rosemary came down to the stone-floored kitchen. There was a note left on the table. "Lunch? Give me a call. Thaw steaks."

Rosemary smiled. No lunch. She did not intend to leave this retreat all day, not even for Beatrice. Weekday lunches suggested business. On such a Tuesday in Minneapolis she might be plying a prospective client with lunch in order to soften him up for her presentation. That is what she was escaping.

The coffee was made. Rosemary took a steaming cup together with some grapes onto the deck and settled down with sensuous content. Beatrice's bird feeders were doing a brisk business, gophers scampered across the redwood deck, and high overhead a hawk hung in the air, poised to make a meal of some unsuspecting animal below. The feeders were suspended from a wire that ran from the silo to a walnut tree thirty yards away, out of reach of squirrels, and Rosemary soon realized she could not identify a fraction of the birds that took serial possession of the perches. In a birdbath a jay bathed itself importantly: dog in the manger, jay in the birdbath.

On her tongue the taste of coffee and fresh grapes set off a small riot of delight. Parisian chefs, eat your hearts out. For such gustatory triumphs they strove and she had hit on this by accident in Fairland.

Forty-five minutes later, she took her third refill to the upper room in search of something to read. A curved bookcase was bright with jackets and the gaudy colors of paperbacks. Trash mostly, romances, thrillers. Rosemary paged through an Agatha Christie, the tried and true. Even if she had read it before, it promised the diversion she sought. Her eye went to the one handsomely bound volume and she took it out. Poetry. Richard Wilbur. *New and Collected Poems.* The back flap of the dustjacket made a marker at page 71. The poem printed there was called "A Shallot."

> The full cloves
> Of your buttocks, the convex
> Curve of your belly, the curved
> Cleft of your sex—
> Out of this corm
> That's planted in strong thighs
> The slender stem and radiant
> Flower rise.

Well. Like everyone else, Rosemary had sometimes

responded to the fruits of the earth, bananas, peaches, gourds, as to a Rorschach test, but it had never occurred to her that a poem might be made of the experience. These eight short lines made her breath catch. She closed the book on its marker and studied the photograph of the poet on the back. Born in 1921? She couldn't believe it. She turned the book, opened it, and saw the written inscription: "To my lady of Shallot. Giorgio."

Rosemary closed the book as if she had been spying on Beatrice's secret life. The inscription and the short poem made it clear that this was no casual gift. Holding the book in both hands, seated on the edge of a chair, Rosemary let her eyes drift westward. She was torn between the thought that it was good Beatrice had found someone and that there was keen pleasure to be had from the loss of love. In her vulnerability, memories of Russ overwhelmed her and Rosemary sat gripping the book, staring beyond time and space, tears running from her eyes.

A good self-indulgent cry, and she enjoyed it to the full. Then she stood, took a deep breath, returned Wilbur to the shelf as she might Beatrice's diary, took the first Miss Marple her hand found and, changed into shorts and halter, went back onto the deck.

She read half the book in one gulp, then napped dangerously in the sun. When she went inside to make a sandwich, the kitchen seemed cool and dark and for a time bright afterimages made it difficult for her to see. When the phone rang she found it by the Braille method.

"Did you get my note?"

"I hope you don't mind about lunch."

"You came down to vegetate. Vegetate. But not tonight. I'll grill steaks."

"Right. How long does it take them to thaw?"

"No, wait, forget it. No tasks for you today. I'll do it in the microwave when I get home. Go be a vegetable."

A shallot? After she hung up, Rosemary had the not unpleasant feeling that she no longer knew Beatrice well, that her old friend had become a stranger, a mysterious stranger, to whom Giorgio gave collections of poetry with one designated as his special message. The slightest twinge of envy mixed with her happiness for Beatrice. Maybe Giorgio was the reason Beatrice had asked her down. Last night, their talk had been catch-up talk and a fair amount of just plain gossip about old Minneapolis friends. And about Stella, of course. It was clear that Beatrice disliked Stella in the extreme. But tonight they would dwell on the future, perhaps, and Beatrice could very well speak of her Giorgio. She had better. Rosemary imagined herself looking at the books, getting up. "What's this? Poetry?" No. Beatrice would know she had already seen the book. So what? It would be a welcome excuse to divulge the heated secret of her lover.

Rosemary actually finished the mystery in midafternoon, propelled by the plot, delighted by Miss Marple, lost in a make-believe world in which, despite bodies and blatherskites, there was order and the promise of a solution to it all.

When she put down the book, she remembered the steaks. She sprang to her feet. When Beatrice mentioned the microwave, Rosemary had shaken her head but said nothing. Rosemary nursed an obscurantist fear of the microwave oven. She had been assured it was nonsense, but she did not like the notion that invisible rays could do in moments what stoves and ovens took far longer to accomplish. Nor did she like the thought that she was eating radiated food.

It was irrational, but real. From the kitchen, a spiral staircase led to a basement room that held the furnace and laundry. And, against the wall, an old-fashioned freezer chest, a relic of the first days of frozen foods. By all logic, her case against the microwave should apply to the freezer as well, but when did fear know logic?

The chest when she opened it gave off a blast of frigid steam. The meat was packaged in butcher paper with the identity of its contents stamped on the outside. Lots of ground round. Ribs. Chucks. Roasts. Rosemary was fascinated and surprised. She had never thought of Beatrice as a big eater. This freezer could supply a family and Beatrice was a single woman. Giorgio? Maybe that was it. Leaning into the chest, Rosemary made a kind of inventory of its contents. Unbelievable. And then she came to the bottom layer.

A different kind of wrapper, black plastic, Scotch-taped. Rosemary lifted one. It didn't feel like meat. It didn't seem frozen, not as the meat had. When she unwrapped one of the packages she did not feel at all as she had examining the book of poetry upstairs. What surprises could there be in a freezer chest.

She peeled the plastic back and said aloud, "My God!"

Neatly marked stacks of one-hundred-dollar bills. The package she held must amount to... Her eyes dropped to the layer of black plastic in the chest.

There was a frozen fortune here.

FIFTEEN

BABS CROSSED the Mendota bridge, swept past Fort Snelling, and took the Crosstown to Lyndale before turning toward downtown. On 50th Street she turned west again and soon was looping around Lake Harriet and then Calhoun. Lake of the Isles was next, one of the rosary of lakes strung like beads on the chain of Minnehaha Creek as it meandered through the city toward the falls. The closer she came to her destination, the slower she drove, restrained by the speed limit on the parkways as well as her own anxiety.

What on earth did she expect to happen when she arrived at the Erickson mansion? The auction was tomorrow. Today was an exhibit day for those contemplating major bids. She had no idea if she would even be admitted to the house. She had no idea if she would even try to get in.

What she did do was circle Lake of the Isles three times, uncertain which of the great houses built in the early part of the century she was looking for. Canoes on the surface of the lake suggested an earlier time, but these were filled not with Indians but with indolent couples paddling away the day in a haze of young love. Babs's middle-aged heart went out to them and the vague yearnings that had taken possession of her since that day in this city months ago when she and Louis had happened upon Stella and Roy rose like an unvoiced cry within her.

On her third circuit of the lake she parked, rolled down the window, and stared out at the canoeists as if this were some strange planet and those pairs another race whose customs were alien to her. She ached with the sense that life had cheated her, that the grand passion for which she was destined had not put in an appearance. To think of Louis now was to want to say aloud that he was not enough, they were not enough, her life was not enough. There had to be more than this.

The canoes were rented by the Park Board. Babs could see from where she sat the dock where they were stored in layered racks, attended by a young Adonis whose golden body was constrained only by sateen swimming trunks. Half a dozen girls also in bathing suits hovered about. Watching them, Babs was struck by the ritual male and female instinctively go through. Perhaps this is true of any species, but to the human is added the burden of consciousness, the need for the attraction to be more than of the flesh. She could not hear what they said, but the lilting voices of the girls alternated antiphonally with the attendant's. It might have been an opera, not least because she did not understand the words.

There came to her then the thought that comes eventually to all, that individuals are the instruments of the species, that those young people whose summer lolling by the lake would seem to them a choice they had made, were actually moved about by the dark roiling of the blood, the fated fixation of the genders for one another. Each of them was looking for a mate, and the sorting out was conscious; but far below the level of planning and hoping and the display and presentation involved in the rite those young people were enacting was the unswerving necessity of Nature. It was Nature that was being served. We have no choice but to be her instruments. Biology rather than romance seemed to provide the basic score for that choir of male and female voices.

The young man slid from its rack a green canoe and, holding it above his head, moved across the dock with it, the female voices rising in response, the carrying of the canoe to the water, the artful easing of it over and down and into the lake a musical phrase that blended movement, the human voice, and a resolving, satisfying splash as the bowed bottom of the craft hit the water. For Babs it was a scene of pagan insouciance, body calling to body, the promise of mindless coupling filling the charged air. There were no comparable moments in her memories of youth. She remembered adolescence as a time of agony, anxiety, self-loathing, insecurity that had created a personality to whom Louis—Louis!—had appeared as a rescuer.

Leaning from the window, her avid stare drifted and she suddenly confronted herself in the rearview mirror. In the millisecond before she knew that face was hers, what did she think of the woman she saw there? A wave of self-disgust swept over her. How did this agony, anxiety, self-loathing, and insecurity differ from her feelings as a girl? Nothing had changed.

The thought that she was no more mature than the girl she had been twenty years before made her sit back and roll up the car window. Each girl down there believed that someone, perhaps that bronzed boy in his blue breechclout, would transform her world. Think of the boy as Louis, Babs said aloud, think of those girls as me. It was a purging, cleansing thought. She tilted the rearview mirror and looked herself in the eye. Prepared to see herself, she had to make an effort to let the signs of middle age reveal themselves. It was not Louis she hated, it was not herself. It was the pressing awareness that the arc of her life had reached an acme and the descent begun.

She had not turned off the engine and the air-conditioning made sitting in the closed car tolerable despite the mounting heat and humidity. In an unlooked-for epiphany Babs saw that it was time's arrow she had been resisting. Birth, infancy, childhood, adolescence, adulthood, age, death. The arrow flew only forward and she had wanted to arrest its flight, restring the bow, start life anew. It could not be done. *Act your age.* She could hear her mother's voice as she remembered the words. It was advice she still needed. Maybe everybody does.

She closed her eyes, pressed her back against the seat, breathed through her nose, and resisted the rising tide of self-pity. For months she had been feeling sorry for herself, encouraging her own discontent, dreaming of infidelity as if she could enjoy an interlude that would bear no relation to her past or future. Childish.

She shifted the car into reverse, opened her eyes, looked out at the tufted islands of the lake, the gray-green water, the reeds along the shore, as if in farewell. She backed carefully out of her place, turned onto the parkway, and completed her circuit of the lake.

This time she knew when she had arrived at the Erickson house; a minor traffic jam had been created by the cars backing into the parking places along the curb. After waiting some ten minutes, Babs was able to pull in and park herself. She had driven to Minneapolis to see the Erickson house and, by God, she was going to do it.

She had dressed for the trip, of course, and entering the great frame house, Babs was glad she was wearing the white dress with a long full skirt, her waist emphasized by a wide red belt. The neckline was daring and she thought ruefully of why she had chosen it. Her shoes matched the belt and earrings. Comfortable yet chic, as a salesgirl might have said.

Young women inside the door distributed catalogues and Babs took one with the sense that she was entering church. Not her own. Claudia considered church bulletins bourgeois. She mailed a newsletter at midweek in which she acquainted her parishioners with her views on current events. Beyond the vestibule was a hallway almost as large as Babs's living room from which a side staircase rose toward a landing where three high windows lifted the eye.

"Cozy little place," a voice said beside her.

He smiled at her over his opened catalogue, a man of perhaps fifty. Babs nodded and looked at her own catalogue.

"Furniture?" he asked.

"I'm not a dealer or anything."

"Let's look upstairs first, defy the traffic pattern."

He started up and Babs followed. She felt less like an intruder with this man. Halfway to the landing he stopped and waited for her to catch up, then they continued together.

"Want to see my room?"

"Your room!"

On the landing he paused, looked up at the high windows, shook his head, then continued.

"I grew up in this house."

He said his name was Erickson, this the family house. He wished he could buy it and save it from this desecration.

"Why don't you?"

One side of his mouth lifted in a grudging smile. "I already own it, my dear. I can't afford to keep it. No one of us can do it alone and we don't get along well enough to hang on to it together."

He took her into the master bedroom, showed her the two baths, his and hers, the dressing rooms, the great bulge of windows with the padded seat. They sat there, pulled back the curtains, looked out at Lake of the Isles. On the opposite side of the lake lovers rented canoes.

"Do you know something? I never went out in a canoe on that lake."

He said it in wondering tones and a sad look came over his face. Canoes were for the nonresidents who invaded the neighborhood on summer weekends, not for Ericksons.

"It must be terrible, the auction."

He looked at her. "What kind of furniture are you looking for?"

She could not tell him that she was here out of curiosity, that she was in Minneapolis for reasons she did not want to think about now. She opened the catalogue in search of an answer to his question.

"I was going to show you my room."

They went into the hall where he hesitated, and for a moment Babs feared he had thought twice about sharing his youthful memories with a stranger. In talking with him, she had put her hand to her throat, embarrassed by her neckline. He could hardly be expected to ignore its invitation. He began to walk briskly and she hurried after him, looking into the rooms on either side of the hall as he did. At the end of the hallway, he stopped at a closed door, eased it open slowly as if he expected it to be occupied, but after looking in he pushed the door open, stepped to one side, and with a sweep of his arm let her enter before him.

The sound of the door closing made her turn. He stood against it, smiling intently at her. The room they were in did not look like a boy's room. There was a single bed, a rocker on an oval rug, a highboy.

"Let's screw."

"What!"

He tipped his head toward the bed but kept his eyes on her. With the hand behind his back, he turned a key. She was locked in with him. It was difficult to feel terror even after his incredible suggestion. On the window seat, he had been such a sympathetic person, and he was so good-looking—short cut hair graying at the sides, gray-green eyes, a cleft in his chin. A romantic figure, selling the family home but only with regret.

"I like that dress."

"Tell me what it was like to grow up here." If she steered him away from herself and the bed everything would be all right. What could happen to her in the middle of the morning in a house open to the public? He moved toward her, slowly, a little boy's smile on his face.

"It wasn't this room exactly." He reached for her hand but she clasped them behind her. A mistake. He ran his finger down the line of her throat and she had to twist away or he would have touched her breast. She started for the door, but he grabbed her and pulled her tightly against him.

"Take it easy." He sounded so calm, so reasonable. It occurred to Babs that this was the kind of situation she had been dreaming of for months. He was pressing her against him and she felt his male readiness. He dipped and brought his lips against her throat. Babs was frightened now. Claudia had given several seminars on rape and Babs had attended them. It had been her pastor's contention that a man is never more vulnerable than when sexually aroused. What could a woman do?

"Knee him," Claudia said. "Bring the knee up into his groin as swiftly and powerfully as you can..."

Babs did it. The effect was magical. He doubled over with a cry of pain and stumbled toward the bed. There was a genuinely puzzled look in his eyes. But Babs was at the door, twisting the key. Pulling open the unlocked door, she burst into the hallway where she collided with Steve Nicodemus.

The bookseller staggered back against the wall. Others coming behind him stopped in astonishment. And then, as if on cue, Erickson came out of the room, an expression of rage dying on his face when he saw the audience.

"Rape," Babs said in strangled tones. "He tried to rape me."

His name wasn't Erickson.

He was an off-duty cop, hired for security purposes, who insisted that Babs had led him on. She was horrified by the suggestion that she prefer charges.

"No!"

This lent credence to the man's claim. Babs was glad to get back to her car. She hoped she would never see Steve Nicodemus again.

SIXTEEN

ROY HUNT could not believe it when Stella, in earshot of everybody and visible to half the diners in the country club dining room, began to shout at him like a shrew. He grabbed her wrist and pulled her away from the doorway, past the bar and out onto the veranda.

"Will you stop pulling me," she hissed at him.

He ignored her. Her voice had dropped with the loss of an audience, but there were people on the veranda and he kept going until they were in the parking lot below the tennis courts, out of sight.

"I could wring your neck," he said.

"You are breaking my wrist."

"What was the meaning of that scene?" He let her go.

"What was the meaning of that scene?" she repeated, mimicking his tone. She drew closer to him, her eyes sparkling with anger. "Why were you so lovey-dovey with Beatrice Dean?"

"Lovey-dovey!"

"Oh Roy, don't act so innocent. I sat on the veranda and watched you fawn over that woman for half an hour."

"You were sitting on the veranda?"

"I was coming across the veranda when I looked in and saw you with her and I was so surprised I just sat down, ordered a drink, and stayed there, wondering how long it would be before you stopped making a spectacle of yourself. Do you know how that woman treated me?''

"Rosemary was there, for God's sake."

"And don't think I won't ask her about it."

That her behavior was the result of jealousy was not an explanation that tempted Roy Hunt. Stella's attitude toward Beatrice, irrational as it was, had a mad logic to it. The better Beatrice performed the job she had been hired to do, the more Stella saw the secretary as a rival for her husband's affections. That had made little sense while George was alive and it made none now that he was dead. But Stella wasn't making much sense in any case.

"Don't you trust me?" he asked.

"Shouldn't I?"

They had arrived at his car as if it were their destination. Perhaps it was. She went to the passenger side and waited for him to open the door. He did. She got in. He went around the car and got behind the wheel. Gripping the wheel, looking straight ahead, he said. "What were you talking with Nicodemus about?"

"Nicodemus! When?"

He turned his wrist and looked at his watch. "Almost exactly an hour and ten minutes ago. I saw you from the golf course..."

"You were spying on me?"

"I was looking for a lost ball."

"Did you find it?"

"No."

"This is what *I* found." She held up a red envelope, one from his own bank, the kind that contained a safe-deposit key.

"Found where?"

"Nicodemus had it."

He took it but his eyes remained on Stella.

"The missing key," she said.

"So what?"

Her mouth fell open in disbelief and she snatched the key from his hand. "You do remember the box was empty when we opened it, don't you? So who emptied it? Neither of us could have."

Aha. He had sensed that she had not really believed him when he told her he could not open a safe-deposit box unless the renter of it produced one of the keys. Had she imagined him taking the money out of George's box and then staging a big show for her when they opened it together?

"You think Nicodemus did?"

"Roy, he's guilty as sin. He actually jumped when I told him I was missing a key. I knew he had it and he did. It was in the drawer of his desk."

"Stella, Nicodemus has a safe-deposit box at the bank too. That key could be his."

For a moment, doubt clouded her eyes, but she shook her head. "Roy, if you were there, if you had seen him react..." She held up a hand to stop him. "Okay, let's check and find out. Either this is George's key or it isn't."

"Even if it is George's key, that doesn't mean Nicodemus actually used it."

"Was George's box empty or not, Roy?"

"But George could have emptied it."

Her eyes narrowed in thought. She shook her head slowly. "No. No, I don't think so."

"He never really liked the idea of the safe-deposit box."

"There is no money hidden in the house."

He started the engine and drove across the parking lot. "Hungry?"

"I'll make us something."

"Stella, we have to take it easy." He turned on his headlights as he went down the driveway to the gate. "We have been through a lot and there is more to get through. This is no time to lose our cool."

"What were you talking with Beatrice about?"

"I was telling Rosemary and Beatrice about the nine holes I had just played."

"Ha."

He let it go. After all, his own suspicions had been aroused when he looked through the woods and saw her seated beside the pool with Nicodemus. They went to her house, where she made a nice fluffy omelet, salad, and iced tea. Then they went upstairs and made love and it wasn't as great as it had been when they used to meet in motels. Even now, he preferred the cabin on Lake Owatonna to the house that still seemed dominated by her father and George.

"When will we get married?" he asked afterward.

"Roy, am I poor?"

"Let's just say you're going to have less than you deserve."

She was going to have less anyway. Not even this house was safe. George had gotten into a situation that jeopardized every part of the business he had taken over from Harald Larson.

"What was he insured for?"

Stella didn't know. Roy felt almost innocent when he realized that neither of them had asked that question before the ice-fishing episode. Of course, they had then imagined Stella would inherit an extensive and profitable concern. Roy knew of his own loan, of course, but had not realized that it was but one of many.

On the ceiling, reflected from a hand mirror that Stella had left face up on the dresser, the light of the moon formed an ectoplasmic presence. The moon itself was a mirror. Roy recalled the barbershops of his boyhood, mirrored wall facing mirrored wall, the infinite repetition of reflected images, long before there was any talk of cloning. Generations? He had mentioned marriage because he wanted to be a father. All these years of loving Stella seemed an investment that should produce a child or two at least.

"We'll have children," he mused aloud.

"What?"

"A girl for you, a boy for me."

"That'll be the day."

He got up on his elbow. "I'm glad you never had his child."

"It was no accident." She said it with satisfaction and Roy ignored the tone of her voice.

"I was never very close to my father."

In the silence she might have been thinking of Harald Larson.

He said, "We'll name the boy Harald."

She stirred beside him. "Are you serious? I mean about children. Because if you are, forget it."

"Don't you want a child?"

"Roy, you know how old I am."

"Old." He pinched her thigh and she rolled away.

"Having a baby after forty is out of the question."

"We'll have a Minneapolis doctor. You could go to Rochester, to Mayo's."

"It would be a medical event. But it isn't going to happen."

He did not address her denials directly. He knew her too well. She would only become more stubborn. So he lay back and spoke of how wonderful it would be with children of their own. Beside him she made wet noises with her mouth, from time to time she tried to speak, but he went on, as if in a trance. Then he fell silent.

"Wonderful," she said. He rolled toward her, to gather her into his arms, but she scooted free. "A boy and his dog, a man and his son. You can teach him all you know." Her voice was heavy with irony. "You can take him fishing, Roy. You can teach him how to fish. Fresh-water fishing. Ice fishing."

The back of his hand caught her in the mouth at the end of an 180-degree arc. She yelped in pain, then began to scream. The hell with it. On his back, looking at the ceiling but ready to defend himself if it came to that, Roy ignored her hysterical tirade. What a bitch, he thought. The sentence repeated itself over and over in his head and then he began saying it aloud. "What a bitch. What a bitch."

She had been moving around the room in her shortie nightgown, screeching at him, but she stopped when he spoke. She was by the dresser. Suddenly there was a whistling sound followed by a crash against the wall. She had thrown the mirror at him. He leaned over the bed and from dozens of fragments scattered about the floor dozens of fragments of moonlight glowed dully.

Silence. She turned on the little dresser lamp and came cautiously around the bed and looked down at the broken mirror.

"My God."

A broken mirror. Seven years' bad luck. Seven more, Roy thought. What had she ever been to him but bad luck? She sat down heavily on the edge of the bed. Did she even remember screaming at him? He put his hand on her bare upper leg and she moved against him.

"Roy, I broke a mirror." She had always been superstitious. Because her father had been. That made it all right.

"You might have hit me with the goddamn thing."

"That was the idea." She tried for a playful tone.

"Lucky me."

"Lucky us if it hadn't broken."

He moved over and she got in beside him, moving warmly against him. What the hell. Well, why not? What did they have beside sex? Later she suggested they spend the next night at the cabin.

"Why?"

"This house is unlucky for us."

PHYLLIS ACTED as if she would have a breakdown when he asked her about Steve Nicodemus's visit. She was flustered to have him monitoring her operation and the more he tried to reassure her it was merely routine the more nervous she got. But he had to check it out.

"You stayed with him while he was in there, I suppose."

She stared at him, eyes wide, trying desperately to remember. "I must have."

He nodded. She should have. Trying to make it sound like a little game, he suggested they run through the routine, forget about Mr. Nicodemus. So they went through the gate and inside.

"I ask for the customer's key after we're here."

Roy handed her the key Stella had filched from Nicodemus. Phyllis took it but just stood there.

"Let's open the box."

"I have to know the number."

He gave her the number of the box he had watched George Arthur fill with seven hundred and fifty thousand dollars in cash. Phyllis, liking this less and less all the time, moved the ladder under the box, climbed it, inserted her key and then the one Roy had given her. At least she tried. It would not fit. She looked down at him, her expression suggesting he had tricked her.

"It doesn't fit."

"Are you sure?"

She made a theatrical effort to put the key into the little door.

"What is the number of Mr. Nicodemus's box?"

"I don't remember." Phyllis looked as if she might cry.

"No reason why you should. Would you go look it up?"

She came carefully down the ladder, then hurried out of the room. From the door above the ladder, the ring of Phyllis's keys still hung.

In a minute she was back. She had brought the Nicodemus card from the file. She handed it to him. He studied it for a moment, nodding as if he were finding just what he wanted, then returned it to her.

"I'll tidy up here, Phyllis. You can go back to your counter."

"Mr. Hunt, if I've done anything wrong..." Her lower lip trembled.

"Wrong? Not at all. Everything is just fine."

Relief broke out on her face. He feared she might fling herself at him and kiss him. She left, too happy to remember her ring of keys. Roy closed the stainless steel gate, got Phyllis's keys, moved the ladder, and opened the Nicodemus box. It did not take a minute to see there was not a quarter of a million dollars of cash in the box. The little red envelope had been slipped down the side. Roy eased it out, closed the box, and put it away. He moved the ladder back to where it had been.

He put Phyllis's key in its slot, then took the key out of the envelope he had found in the Nicodemus box. It slipped easily into the slot. Roy turned the key from Phyllis's ring of keys and then the key he had found in the Nicodemus box, and opened the door containing George's box. Still standing on the ladder, he flipped the box open. Still empty. Of course.

He closed it up, came down, and leaned on the table in the center of the room, thinking. It was no problem to imagine how it could have happened. Nicodemus asks to open his safe-deposit box. Phyllis takes him in, opens it, gives him his box, and leaves him. She also leaves the master key. Nicodemus is thus able to open the Arthur box and remove the cash.

So now he knew.

The question that arose was whether or not he would tell Stella.

SEVENTEEN

THE POINT of organization is that it enables a business to go on operating despite changes in personnel. That Arthur Enterprises continued to thrive months after the disappearance and death of its president was due less to organization than to Beatrice Dean. But then she had been part of George's organizational plan.

It was odd that she still felt close to him at work, as if he were somehow still there, as indeed he was in terms of what he had created in the past.

"Further expansion here is impossible," he had told her, sitting on her deck, his narrowed eyes looking into the distance.

Was he thinking of taking seriously the bids to buy him out that came regularly, most recently from Japan and Britain, the dollar coming home to roost?

They talked about it. He was not enthusiastic.

"Beatrice, when I came here my idea of money was money. Cash. I paid money for things, buildings, land, an ongoing business. If I sold now I wouldn't get my price in money. Nobody has money anymore. Wealth is certificates, pieces of paper, numbers on a printout."

She came to realize how old-fashioned he was. He did not like Wall Street, venture capital, stockholders for whom a company was little more than a name, a logo, an entry on the exchange.

"Two things will kill this country, Beatrice. The computer and this." He held up a plastic credit card.

She looked up to him, metaphorically but literally too. She had never before tipped her head back to look at a man's face. His was a granite face, monumental, ready for Mount Rushmore. She felt in the presence of primal energy when she was with him, whether at the office or at the silo.

"Do you know how many chapter elevens there are in this country alone each year?"

He did. There was no longer any shame in bankruptcy. People spent imaginary money, got hopelessly into debt, filed Chapter 11 and started over again. No credit cards could be used at the AE stations at the northern and southern entries to Fairland.

"Not that the dollar is what it used to be. If it weren't so damned impractical, I'd go for gold. You can't go wrong with gold."

When he held her in her circular bed she felt small, a new sensation for her. Thoughts of him with his wife tried to form in her mind, but with the strength of long habit she resisted them. Her fundamental outlook was that Stella did not exist. She was less real than the certificates and numbers on the computer printouts George hated. Or no more real. She was an asset. She had been. She was no more.

"If I hadn't married Larson's daughter, it would have been a hostile takeover. In a town this size, goodwill is everything. People actually congratulated me for rescuing Larson's daughter as well as his company."

Beatrice never told him what she knew about Stella. Each of them, husband and wife, thought to have done the other a favor by marrying. There had never been love. Stella had gone on loving her former fiancé. In a real sense, it was Roy Hunt she was married to. And Beatrice had become George Arthur's true love.

"I never want to leave this place," he would say when the time came for him to go, and he meant it. He loved her converted silo. Like most businessmen he was a dreamer, and he dreamt of settling into isolated obscurity with her and living happily ever after. But because he was a businessman he also meant to bring it about.

It was Roy Hunt who inadvertently suggested what he had been seeking. Despite his theories, George's loans had always been computer transfers, some keys punched at his bank, an entry appearing at another, the deal consummated. But one could ask that borrowed money be money. Of course. Why not? It was a way of keeping the deal absolutely quiet until it went through.

"Not even you, Roy. I promised."

"As long as I have collateral you can take the money and flee to Tahiti."

An uncharacteristic joke and one that gave George pause. Beatrice did not try to tell him Roy's remark meant nothing. He would come to that realization by himself. She wanted to be led by him, not to lead. She had always despised weak men and now she had a strong one.

When he told her about his wife urging him to put cash in a safe-deposit box, Beatrice waited. She did not have to tell him to be wary.

"Good old Roy Hunt can fix it up, isn't that wonderful? Roy Hunt, the friend of her childhood."

Did he suspect something? If he did, it was beneath his notice. Why should he care what Stella did?

Beatrice was not surprised to learn that he had that much cash in his home. He already had a comparable amount in the office safe, the safe in his office, that is, the one he had put in after Beatrice came. The office was carpeted wall to wall; high windows looked in two directions, toward town and toward the river. His desk was so placed that, seated at it, he faced the river. His chair moved on the large plastic mat Harald Larson had used and that he had kept despite redecoration. The man who laid the carpet had not detected the artful inlay George had made himself to conceal the safe in the floor. Afterward, George cut a flap in the carpet; the desk chair mat went over it. Only George Arthur and Beatrice had the combination to the safe. It was there he meant to put the cash he borrowed against the company on the excuse that he was going to build, going to merge, going to expand in various ways, each loan predicated on a different supposed project.

George brought the money to the bank in a briefcase on the day he had ceremoniously entered into the plan Stella and Roy had devised to keep his cash secure and out of the reach of the IRS. Two days later, Beatrice transferred it to a box rented in her own name. The safe in the office meanwhile filled with money borrowed from a multitude of sources. Three and a half million dollars. They were waiting for five hundred thousand more. When that came, they would leave.

It was the dead of winter. They would drive south in a rented car, rent a boat, and cruise the eastern shore of Mexico for a month or more before making port at Sarasota. Beatrice had bought in the name of a corporation formed for the purpose the place on Siesta Key where they would stay until the spirit moved them to go.

"I wish we could move the silo there," he said.

With him, anywhere, anyplace, was all right with her. He still seemed surprised to hear how much she loved him. The money did not matter. Sometimes she imagined them going away without the money, starting over elsewhere. They did not need four million dollars to be happy. Four thousand would be enough. George was not that romantic. So they waited a week more in order to get the five hundred thousand that would round it off at four million.

In the meantime he went ice fishing with Roy Hunt.

From the beginning she had known that George was dead. Stella knew it too, and so did Roy Hunt, because they had killed him. But they had done it in so stupid a way that they had to wait four months before they could even open his safe-deposit box.

She knew that they hadn't. If they had, they would sooner or later have come to the office to see if he had transferred the money there. By then, Beatrice had taken the money home, wrapped it, and put it into her freezer beneath the meat. She was certain George would have approved. But like Stella and Roy she was immobilized until the body was found in the spring. It crossed her mind to take the money and do what she and George had planned to do together, but, all she would find on Siesta Key was loneliness and she had that here in the silo. As for the money, the point was to prevent its falling into Stella's hands. Wait until she discovered the condition of the company. She and Roy would find they had committed murder to no advantage.

That had seemed punishment enough, but Beatrice was not privy to their reaction when they found the safe-deposit box empty. Roy Hunt, on behalf of the bank, came to inquire into the security for his loan. He was surprised to find others coming for the same purpose. Beatrice called a meeting of the firm's creditors and more or less presided as recording secretary.

"But where is the money?" a Minneapolis banker asked, addressing the question to the other lenders. They turned to Beatrice.

"Mr. Arthur kept cash in a safe-deposit box at Mr. Hunt's bank."

Roy's reaction told Beatrice he had discovered the empty box. There was some satisfaction to be had from watching Stella's lover attempt to look knowledgeable and ignorant at the same time.

"In my bank, Miss Dean? I'd have to check, but I don't think so."

"In your bank. Mr. Arthur was quite definite about it."

A box not registered in his name. If Roy Hunt admitted to that he would have to open the box, and he knew there was nothing in it. He pulled a phone toward him across the shiny surface of the conference room table. He got through, put the question, asked to be called back.

The phone rang ten minutes later. Roy looked up the table at Beatrice.

"He had no box with us, Miss Dean. If he meant to rent one, he never got around to it."

She said nothing. There was nothing to prevent the vultures from moving in now. Foreclosures were in the air.

"Several Japanese firms and one British company approached Mr. Arthur in recent months. Their offers were very attractive and he would have been kept on as well. His reaction was to raise money for expansion."

Interest in the makers of those bids was avid.

"Mr. Inagake called again a week ago, to express his sorrow at the death of Mr. Arthur."

George had not planned it quite this way, but he was confident that in the end everyone would be content. The bankers would get their money back, everything would be bought up by the Japanese, but everything would go on as before.

"But without us," he added, smiling down at her.

Now Beatrice had been confronted by a wholly unlooked-for eventuality—that she would go on without George. It had changed her attitude toward the three and a half million dollars in her freezer chest.

The money was no longer a passport to a new life for her and George. Beatrice would stay on in Fairland for a decent interval and then go. Or perhaps stay, live at the silo, and... And what? Dear God, how bleak the future was. That was why she had asked Rosemary to come stay with her. If only they could stay together permanently. Beatrice could face the prospect of life alone if she could do it with Rosemary at her side.

Now the money represented revenge. It was the penalty exacted from Stella for cheating on George from the very outset of their marriage.

While George was alive, Stella almost never came to the office and after that awful day in February when the long vigil began, she continued to keep her distance from her husband's business affairs. It would have looked unseemly, presuming on her widow's status, wondering what she was now worth. Of course, Roy Hunt could have given her some information, but it would have been inaccurate. How could Roy know that George had decided to liquidate the business by making it hostage to loans that, if called in, would necessitate selling off the assets of Arthur Enterprises one by one?

Then one day Beatrice came in to find Stella seated behind George's desk, a pile of folders at her elbow and one open before her. She did not look up.

"Can I be of any help?" Beatrice asked.

"I'll let you know." Stella kept her eyes on the paper before her.

During the morning, Beatrice was told that Mrs. Arthur had requested her folder from personnel. A buzz from George's office at eleven. Beatrice ignored it. It sounded again and again. After a futile ten minutes, Stella stormed into her office.

"Are you deaf?"

Beatrice did not look up from the letters she was signing. Stella marched up to her desk and snatched a letter from Beatrice but Beatrice's hand closed on Stella's wrist. A momentary struggle and then Beatrice relinquished her grasp.

Stella's eyes blazed.

"You are fired!"

"Mrs. Arthur, since I do not work for you, you cannot fire me."

"I own this company. I want you out of here."

"You still can't fire me."

She had a personal contract with George, and it had a year to run. Not that she explained this to Stella. There was too much satisfaction in watching her apoplectic reaction to what she clearly regarded as a mutiny.

Stella did not return after noon. When Beatrice went out to her car at five-thirty she had four flat tires. She went back inside and called the AE garage, and while she waited for them to pump up her tires, she tried to think as dispassionately as she could of ways to punish Stella for this childish yet malicious prank.

But it was obvious what she should do. She telephoned Sheriff Ewbank and told him, speaking in a low voice, that Stella Arthur and Roy Hunt had been lovers for years and had good reason to get rid of George.

TODAY WHEN she left work her tires were full. She began to sing on the drive home, surprising herself. How long had it been since she had sung? Since February. And why was she happy? Because Rosemary awaited her, and she would grill steaks, and the two of them would talk the night away.

EIGHTEEN

DRIVING BACK from Minneapolis Wednesday night, the van loaded with books from the auction, Steve couldn't make up his mind whether or not to tell Mabel about what had happened at the Erickson house on Tuesday. In the event, he didn't have to decide. When he got home, Mabel awaited him, eager to tell him of Babs Poeglin's big adventure in Minneapolis.

"A man attacked her," Mabel said in a whisper she had difficulty keeping under control.

"No kidding."

"She heard us talking about the Erickson auction and went there, and upstairs this man forced her into a room." Mabel paused for effect. "Nothing happened."

"That sounds like a lot."

"She wondered if you'd heard of it."

"It happened upstairs?"

"In a bedroom. He claimed to be one of the Ericksons and offered to show her the room he had had as a boy. Once inside, he locked the door and tried to..."

"I spent most of my time in the library."

"The worst part, Babs said, was the skepticism she faced when she escaped the room. Even when the man admitted he wasn't an Erickson. He was on the security detail!"

Steve certainly wasn't going to contradict Babs's version of what had happened. Was it possible that she was so excited when she dashed into the hallway that she hadn't recognized him as the man she ran into? He doubted it, but what did he know? No one had ever tried to rape him.

"Babs said a thing like that makes you see your life differently. I mean, what we already have is so wonderful, yet how easily it could be lost."

"She's become a philosopher."

"You didn't hear anything about it?"

"I stayed in the room after Dolan followed her into the hallway. They didn't catch me."

"Steve!" She dug a finger into his ribs. She drew back. "How did you know his name was Dolan?"

"Well, it wasn't Erickson."

"You did know the story already, didn't you?"

"Not the details."

"Would you have told me if I didn't already know?"

"We'll never know."

THE REST OF the week was devoted to unpacking the Arthur collection and distributing it on the shelves and then getting to work on what he had picked up at the Erickson auction. On Friday, working in the store, he heard Babs outside talking with Mabel. He stayed where he was. Twenty minutes later, Mabel opened the door.

"Babs and I are going to the art fair in Riverfront Park. Want to come along?"

It was a pro forma request. He said he had best keep on with what he was doing.

"Hi, Steve," Babs called over Mabel's shoulder.

"Hi, Babs."

The door closed.

He had bid on everything Erickson had in religion and philosophy, acting on a remark he had overheard years ago concerning Erickson's interest in philosophy. It had been at a lecture at the University of Minnesota, a very talkative person behind him who, as they waited for the lecturer to be introduced, chatted nonstop, presumably to someone he was with. Despite the annoyance of that knowing chatter, the mention of Erickson's philosophy collection stuck in Steve's mind. Only two others bid for it, and he was successful. Unpacking it, he found more stuff in the Scandinavian languages than he had noticed when he inspected the library. A first edition of Kierkegaard's papers, much used, scribbled annotations by the owner from whom Erickson had bought it. As he unpacked the books, Steve thought of putting together a catalogue of the Scandinavian stuff, a special-interest offer.

With that possibility in mind, he entered each item twice on the computer, once in the general inventory and again in a special file.

Saturday morning he received a letter with the address printed in pencil. Local postmark. He removed his feet from the lower drawer of his desk and opened the envelope carefully. Often such envelopes had brought inquiries that led to real finds. When he saw the two little red envelopes inside, his first reaction was disappointment. Then he realized what they were. Safe-deposit keys.

Nothing about the envelope told him who had sent it, but in the course of the next hour, seated uneasily and frowning at his desk, he arrived at several inescapable conclusions.

He had received in the mail the key to his own safe-deposit box and, unless he was very much mistaken, the key that had fallen out of one of George Arthur's books.

But that was the key he had put for safekeeping in his safe-deposit box.

Someone, therefore, had opened his safe-deposit box.

His copy of that key had been in his desk and it was no longer there.

Whoever had taken his key had opened his box, found George Arthur's key, and mailed both to him.

Stella Arthur. Somehow she had managed to do what he had lacked the nerve even to try, open someone else's safe-deposit box.

But why had she sent the key to him? She had teased him with the silly notion that a clock key might be found among the books. How could she have guessed he had the key? The teasing had come first, before the phony interest in Edna St. Vincent Millay. But why would she send her husband's key back to him?

Several times since buying George Arthur's books, Steve had half regretted it because of Stella. Now he wished he had never heard of the woman or her husband's books. He had been drawn into something and he did not understand what it was. What had kept him from trying to open Arthur's safe-deposit box, morality aside, was the fear of what it would do to his professional reputation. Now, after all these years in the business, his reputation was in Stella Arthur's hands, and the way she was acting indicated she meant to use the power he had given her.

He got up and shuffled up and down the aisles of the store. There were no customers, he did not open until ten, and he walked among his books with the growing fear that he had put in jeopardy what he and Mabel had spent their lives building up. There had to be something he could do, but he didn't know what.

When he had it, he did not think much of the idea, but it was dumb enough to work. The first thing he had to know was whether or not he was right in assuming that Stella was behind this. It was bad enough to have someone send those keys, but it would be far worse not to know who it was. How can you deal with an unknown enemy?

He wrapped the copy of Edna St. Vincent Millay, typed her address on a bookstore label, and drove to the post office. He weighed it himself, bought the required number of stamps from a machine, and dropped it into an outside mail receptacle. He drove home unsure that what he had done was wise, but sure it would smoke Stella out. He had to find out what her game was.

On Monday morning she came to the bookstore.

"Thank you for the poems," she said.

He remained silent.

"Did you receive the key?"

"You sent two of them. I'm only missing one."

"Don't be cute, Mr. Nicodemus. You know where I found the key that does not belong to you. You also know that the box it opens is empty. A great deal of money is missing. I want it."

"Rosemary Burnet mentioned that your husband sometimes concealed money in his books. I haven't found any. I did find this."

He handed her the key that had fallen from one of George Arthur's books. She shook her head.

"Not good enough. Where is the money?"

"I told you. I've found none."

"The money that was in the safe-deposit box." She spoke each word with hissing distinctness. "Seven hundred and fifty thousand dollars."

"My God."

"Haven't you counted it?"

"I don't have any money of yours, Mrs. Arthur, let alone a fortune."

"That key opens the box."

He had laid it on the desk before her. They both looked at it, and it occurred to Steve that not only was he innocent of the deed she suggested, however much he had dreamed of perpetrating it, there was no way it could be known that he had not just discovered the key he was presenting to her now.

"Then I'm glad to have found it for you. It fell out of one of the books . . ."

"Stop it!" She leapt to her feet and leaned over the desk, a wild look in her eyes. "You hid that key in your own safe-deposit box."

"Are you confessing to breaking into my box, Mrs. Arthur?"

Suddenly he felt in charge, cleansed of the crazy desires that had plagued him ever since he found that stupid key. He was invulnerable. He had done nothing wrong and clearly she had. In her widened eyes, the same thoughts seemed to form. Her mouth opened but no sound came out.

"You shit!" she screamed. "Where is my money?"

Nicodemus started to get to his feet but Stella, her face twisted in rage, shoved at the desk. The force of it knocked him backward and then she kept pushing. Off balance, Steve fell back against the shelves holding his rare books. The shelves gave, tottered, lost their balance, and began to fall backward. But the books themselves began to fall on Steve, bouncing off his head, his shoulders, burying Nicodemus.

By the time he got out from under the books and to his feet, she was gone, the bells above the door jangling. Steve addressed the closed door.

"You bitch," he said, almost thoughtfully. "You spoiled wicked bitch."

Then he took the key, put it into an envelope, and mailed it to its owner, George Arthur.

NINETEEN

THE MEAT tasted like money, or so Rosemary imagined when Beatrice came home and grilled the steaks that had come from the freezer. If Beatrice had any inkling Rosemary had discovered those packages of cash—she had stopped counting after nineteen and did not dare to speculate what the total might be—she gave no sign of it.

"Oh good," she said when she came in from the garage and saw the thawed steaks on the kitchen counter. "I'll change and get started on dinner."

"What can I do?"

"Can you start the charcoal?"

"I've never done it."

"Better do the salad then."

Rosemary did the salad. When Beatrice came down the spiral stairs, stunning in white shorts and a plaid blouse, Rosemary realized how proportionate this place was to Beatrice's size. It seemed unfair that, this side of the NBA, there wasn't a man large enough for Beatrice. But basketball players and men the size of Uncle George were in short supply.

Uncle George. How little Beatrice had spoken of George since his body was found. It had not been lost upon Rosemary that her friend had a more than ordinary devotion to her boss. The move to Fairland had been made to take the job with him, but even before that Beatrice had obviously had a crush on George

Arthur. Rosemary wondered if George had even suspected what her feelings were toward him.

"What did George think of this place?" Rosemary asked when they were seated side by side at the redwood table on the deck and ate the delicious steaks that tasted like money.

"He loved it. His first impulse was to want to buy it from me."

During the remodeling and redecorating, Beatrice had consulted no wishes but her own—why would she?—which is why the silo was perfect for her, the height of the ceilings proportionate to her height, the sink and stove and other appliances not requiring her to stoop over them. Beatrice's large circular bed and the beds in the two guest rooms were oversize, specially made. Rosemary felt undersized in the silo, but then Beatrice must have felt gigantic in most settings. George would have found the dimensions of the converted silo perfect.

The dishes had been taken in and they were back at the table sipping coffee, when Beatrice said, as if there had been no interval since Rosemary mentioned her uncle, "We were lovers, Rosie."

There may be books of etiquette that provide advice on how to answer such a remark, but Rosemary did not know them. She held her coffee in both hands, looked out at the river, and did not know what to say. Giorgio. Of course. She put down her mug and laid a hand on Beatrice's arm.

"You are the only one I would tell."

Rosemary nodded. "I'm glad you did." Was she? She didn't feel glad. An enormous sadness suddenly swept over her, the sadness she had felt when she knew that Russ had been taken from her and life would have to be lived without him. She put her arm around Beatrice's waist, laid her head on her friend's shoulder, and burst into tears.

They did not talk of it again until several hours later when they were in the upper room. In search of distraction, they had proved to themselves there was nothing worth watching on television. Beatrice put on some Brahms, drew her legs up under her on the couch, and looked across at Rosemary.

"If you want to ask me anything, go ahead."

The question that had throbbed in Rosemary's mind all afternoon nearly leapt from her lips. *What is all that money doing in the freezer?* Thinking it now, it did not seem to be a change of subject. It was as if she already knew whose money that was and even had an intimation why it was there.

"When did it start?"

"Not right away. I was here for years before he suspected what I felt for him. Rosie, I loved him from the first time you introduced us. But it was this place that broke the ice. He came here, he sat on the deck, there wasn't the office to obstruct things. It happened. It was meant to happen."

"Stella never suspected?"

Beatrice shook her head. "I don't think anyone knew."

How awful it must have been for Beatrice during those months before the body was found. Rosemary tried to recall conversations with her friend during that period, but she could remember nothing special in Beatrice's manner.

"You wouldn't have mentioned this while he was alive."

"Rosie, I was certain he was dead last February. What was the alternative? Running away and disappearing. He would have taken me if that is what he had done. No, I knew he was dead. I knew he had been killed."

"Killed?"

"I came to Fairland to work for George when I found out that Stella was unfaithful to him. With Roy Hunt. It had been going on for years. I hired a detective. I wanted to be sure. That made George fair game for me, and I meant to have him if I could."

"You think Stella killed George?"

"She was at least an accomplice. Even if Roy Hunt actually did it."

"Do you know this?"

The Brahms was done and Beatrice replaced it with melancholy Irish ballads. "I don't know it the way I know she was having an affair with Roy."

"Was that the motive, their affair?"

"I don't know."

"Did George know?"

"I never told him. I didn't want him to turn to me because Stella was unfaithful."

Beatrice had a complicated moral code Rosemary did not pretend to understand. What she could understand was a total love for a man, a love that did not stop when the man ceased to be. Beatrice's confession brought them closer together, made them more alike than they had ever been. How similar their situations were, a lover slain, a lonely future ahead, but one freely accepted. What substitute could there be for true love?

Rosemary stayed on at the silo. Her Minneapolis office was as close as the phone; she had no major projects on her calendar and was not yet in a mood to go in pursuit of them. She needed a rest and staying with Beatrice in the silo was perfect. In the evenings, Beatrice confided more and more of her love for George, and Rosemary listened willingly. How difficult it must have been to keep all this quiet after George was dead.

Was it possible that Beatrice was right, that Stella and Roy had murdered George? Sheriff Ewbank's visit made it seem less fantastic.

It was midmorning when Rosemary looked out the kitchen window to see the sheriff's car come to a stop in the turnaround in front of the garage. Her first reaction was fear. He knew about the money in the freezer. Rosemary did not want to talk to the sheriff about the money or anything else. She decided not to answer the door. But Sheriff Oscar Ewbank was a persistent man. He rang the bell, waited, then walked around the silo, inspecting it from the outside. He went back to the door then and, having rung the bell, began to pound on the door.

"Rosemary Burnet," he shouted. "It's Sheriff Ewbank."

So he knew she was there. It gave her no choice but to let him in.

If the sheriff wondered why it had taken her so long to answer the door, he said nothing. Even with his wide-brimmed hat, massive belly, and the metal and leather look of him, he seemed small in Beatrice's house.

"Never been in here," he said, taking off his hat. "Not since it stopped being a silo anyway."

"Beatrice isn't here."

"Working?"

He started up the spiral staircase but Rosemary laid a hand on his arm.

"We can talk here."

"I'd like to see what she's done to the place."

"You'll have to ask her to show you around, then. I am only a guest."

"You think she'd mind?"

"I would mind."

He saw that she meant it and came down the two steps he had mounted.

"I came to talk to you."

"How did you know I was here?"

"Your car is here."

Rosemary dropped her chin and looked at him. "You can see through garage walls?"

He laughed. "One of my deputies noticed it the other day."

The first day she had left the car outside the garage but some very healthy birds had convinced her that Beatrice was right to say she should put it in the garage.

"What did you want to see me for?"

"It's about your aunt Stella Arthur."

"Yes?"

The bright little eyes darted about her face. What an annoying man he was. Rosemary did not like the suggestion that nothing escaped the eyes of the sheriff and his men, she did not like the persistence with which he had managed to get into the house, she liked even less his effort to inspect the house uninvited. But even if none of those things had annoyed her, she disliked enormously the way he studied her after mentioning Stella.

"No one has seen her for two days."

"No one?"

"She hasn't been home."

"Has she been reported missing?"

He seemed to decide not to lie. "I have been trying to reach her for two days. She hasn't been home."

"Maybe she doesn't want to talk with you."

"Why wouldn't she?"

"I can think of several reasons. But whatever her reasons, I share the sentiment. I'm going to ask you to leave."

"Have you seen your aunt in the past two days?"

"Sheriff, I see no reason to answer these questions."

"You're not worried about her?"

"Because you haven't seen her in two days? No."

"Maria Elena is worried."

Rosemary did not rise to what she was sure was bait. The maid Maria Elena might be manipulated by this bumpkin of a sheriff, but she refused to be. She went to the back door and opened it, waiting for Oscar Ewbank to leave. After a moment's hesitation, he went out. From his car, he called back over his shoulder.

"If you see her, tell her I'm looking for her."

Rosemary closed the door without answering. Suddenly the thought of all that money in the freezer sent a chill through her, as if the sheriff's visit had been about the money rather than Stella.

Last night, Rosemary had felt sure that eventually Beatrice would tell her about the money, explain where it had come from and why it was there. It had even occurred to her that Beatrice might have asked her to take out the steaks in the hope that she would discover the money. Could anyone come upon that amount of money and not mention it? Maybe Beatrice had waited all last night for her to bring it up.

Well, eventually the subject would arise. Confiding in her about George had taken a lot more courage than talking about money.

In the afternoon, Beatrice called.

"You sound sleepy."

"I fell asleep on the deck."

"In the sun!"

"Not when I woke up."

"Be careful." A pause. "Oscar Ewbank came by here today asking about Stella."

"He was here this morning, Beatrice."

"Did you let him in?"

"For a few moments. He left when I asked him to."

"Have you talked with Stella?"

"No. She doesn't know I'm here. The last time I saw her she was quarreling with Roy Hunt at the club. Beatrice, the sheriff has been talking with Maria Elena, who probably panicked at the sight of all that leather and metal. He must have a hundred bullets stuffed in that silly belt of his. Maria Elena would tell him anything he wants to hear."

"I'll be home shortly after five."

"Want me to take anything out of the freezer?"

A noticeable pause.

"Why don't we order pizza?"

"Good."

TWENTY

OSCAR EWBANK had lived most of his forty years knowing that the initial reaction to his physical appearance was negative. He had always been shorter and fatter and more pustular than his schoolmates; he had been awkward, a miserable athlete, a zero where girls were concerned. He himself avoided mirrors and had kept only a few photographs of himself, those in which he was with parents or relatives. Nonetheless, Oscar had been senior class president, a Big Man on Campus at the Mankato branch of the University of Minnesota, was in his third term as elected sheriff, and a major force in the Democratic Farmer Labor Party. His life, he sometimes thought, was a triumph over the impediment of his unprepossessing appearance.

He expressed himself in that way. When he was young, the results of IQ tests were a closely guarded secret, not least from the ones tested, but Oscar had subsequently become aware of his intellectual capacities. Indeed, considered from the point of view of what he was capable of doing, his position as sheriff of Olson County did not fulfill his potential. He was heavily overqualified for his job. The explanation was simple. His father had been sheriff of Olson County for a quarter of a century and when Oscar was asked to run he willingly left his office in the Minnesota Department of Highways. He had never regretted the decision.

A uniform is the best way to conceal unattractive peculiarities, and by and large Oscar's first impressions were more favorable when he was rigged up in the sheriff outfit that was at least in part of his own design. To the knowledgeable it might conjure up shades of Hermann Goering, but there were few knowledgeable people in Olson County. The cowboy hat was risky, veering toward parody, but for the most part it served its purpose. There were exceptions, of course, usually women. Exceptions like Rosemary and Beatrice.

Oscar would have liked to look around the converted silo but Rosemary had been perfectly right not to allow it. Most people regarded a uniform as the equivalent of a police warrant, and Oscar seldom encountered resistance when he wanted to enter a house. He might have persisted if it had not been just a matter of curiosity. It was ridiculous to think that Stella Arthur would be hiding in the home of a woman she despised.

"I want to take possession of my husband's place of business," Stella had announced, standing in front of his desk, glaring at him as if the sheriff were preventing her from accomplishing her wish.

"Are you the heir?"

"Heir? As far as we know, George is missing and that is all."

All? This had been in April. Oscar could see why George might want to put a lot of miles between himself and his wife, but the chances that George was only another missing person were slim. On the other hand, no one was in a mood to declare a man dead because he hadn't been seen for a month and a half.

Bessie, the sheriff's Labrador retriever, lifted her muzzle from the floor and regarded Stella with large liquid eyes. It takes a bitch to know one? Perhaps. Oscar talked to Bessie a lot but she had never answered yet.

Stella's visit had been Oscar's first inkling that something very funny was involved in George Arthur's disappearance. From the beginning he had thought Roy Hunt was kidding when he said he had taken George ice fishing for the first time in the middle of the worst snowstorm of the year. And when was the last time you heard of someone falling through a hole in the ice made for fishing? Bessie didn't answer. It was the implausibility of that happening that led Oscar to list George as a missing person. But if George was missing, he knew perfectly well the consternation his going had caused; maybe that had been part of the motive.

Now Beatrice Dean was preventing Stella from taking over Arthur Enterprises. It was almost as if the secretary—or administrative assistant, as she corrected him—expected her boss to return and Stella did not.

Stella had been in the cabin on Lake Owatonna on that stormy February day when her husband had gone out with Roy Hunt on his first and last ice-fishing adventure. When Oscar arrived, he talked with Roy first and then went into the main room of the cabin where Stella sat before the fire.

"George built it," she said.

"The cabin?"

She looked up at him as if he had meant to offend her. "The fire. Before he went out on the ice."

"And never came back," Oscar said sadly, lowering himself into a chair. This had the effect of making Stella spring out of hers.

"Aren't you going to search for him?"

"Roy has already taken some of my men out to the shack."

Oscar went out to the scene then, not expecting any help from Stella. Her story was the same as Roy's except that she had remained in the cabin.

"I watched them go out together. Roy went out first, then came back for George."

"Why?"

"George wouldn't have known one shack from another."

"I meant, why was Roy out there alone in the first place?"

She looked at him. He half expected her to tell him it was a good question. "Seeing that everything was all right, I guess."

Speaking with Stella and Roy, Oscar had the advantage of knowing that the two of them had been carrying on for years. An advantage, or disadvantage, of law enforcement is that you become privy to the nonindictable misbehavior of so many respectable citizens. Oscar hadn't been in office a month before he first heard of Stella and Roy spending the afternoon in a motel. He kept his own eyes open after that and, sure enough, sometimes discreetly, sometimes not, Stella and Roy got together regularly.

It seemed a reckless, foolish thing for both of them. Roy Hunt was a more successful banker than even his father had been, and it made no sense to risk his reputation in this way. Stella risked, if possible, even more. George had bought and rebuilt the empire

Harald Larson had built, he was a valued resource of the community. Moreover, he was what Oscar Ewbank would have been if he had been allowed to choose his appearance: tall, handsome, astute, a man's man. A proud man. If he learned what Stella was doing he would figure out a way to cut her off without a penny.

The plot thickened when the number of loans George had taken out became clear. Oscar's source here was a St. Paul banker he had gone to school with and who had been in the Highway Department with Oscar. He had phoned Oscar when he read of George Arthur's ice-fishing mishap.

"Is he dead, Oscar?"

"We haven't found a body."

"Do you expect to?"

"Not before the spring thaw."

"There's no doubt he drowned?"

"Of course there's doubt he drowned. He could have skipped out of that shack, continued on across the lake, reached the highway there, and just kept going."

"Why?"

"I don't know."

"He was planning a major expansion, Oscar."

"Tell me about it."

George had taken a very large loan from the St. Paul bank and that was not compatible with the theory that he had used the cover of the storm to walk off and disappear. There were other large loans too, it emerged, but then George's body was found and that stopped the speculation.

Toward spring, Oscar stopped by the cabin on Lake Owatonna from time to time, standing on the porch and looking out at the ice. It had gone from black to gray and then became slushy. Then one day, the lake was free of ice. Roy Hunt was already out on the lake when Oscar got there. Looking for the body of his old friend? Bessie thought about it. But they hadn't been friends, George and Roy. In fact, Roy had been playing around with George's wife. Oscar would not have been a lawman if he had not considered the possible implications.

The illicit couple lure their victim to an isolated area—and what more isolated than a fishing shack on a frozen lake in a blizzard?—do away with him, and live happily ever after. The difficulty was that Roy and Stella did not seem to be living happily ever after. It was almost as if George had anticipated what they were up to and had ensured that they would be in for a sad surprise. George had even taken out a second mortgage on the house, so that there was nothing of his personal property or Arthur Enterprises not encumbered with debt.

It made no sense to think that George Arthur of all people would have gone passively to the slaughter, contenting himself with making certain that his assassins would not profit from their deed.

"You would think he was getting ready to run away," Oscar told Bessie, who listened attentively as always to what her master said.

Much food for thought, and Oscar didn't object to that. It was seldom enough that his job taxed his mind in the slightest. He had reconciled himself to it by making a virtue out of its boredom. There are worse things than jobs that do not engage the mind. It left him free for other things. Among the accomplishments Oscar had acquired during the ample leisure time that was his was a knowledge of Italian and a devotion to the sonnets of Petrarch. He had put several of these into English and two had been published in a literary quarterly that was published on the Mankato campus. One of his complaints about Nicodemus's bookstore was that he had so little in foreign languages.

"I can get hold of anything a customer wants," Steve had replied. Not that Oscar had let the bookseller know he was the putative customer wanting works in Italian.

Oscar had bought a thing or two from Nicodemus, unobtrusively. Nicodemus took the purchases to be busman's holiday stuff, but Oscar had a fairly impressive little collection on the function of the sheriff through history, the Arabic origin of the name, the relation of that to the term *shire,* and so on.

But the Stella Arthur and Roy Hunt shenanigans had, from the time he first became aware of them, promised trouble of the kind a constabulary is needed for. Now the wronged husband was dead. And there were others who had known of this prolonged infidelity, at least one other. The phone call provided an excuse for Oscar to bring the matter up with Louis Poeglin.

The physician's reaction had been surprising. He went red with anger, and Oscar momentarily feared it was the messenger rather than the message that had angered Louis. If Oscar had anticipated a long discussion of the matter he would have been disappointed. Louis was suddenly eager to call it a night, and he left for home within the half hour. Rather than annoyance, Oscar felt admiration for the doctor. The world would be a better place if we were less quick to believe the worst of others. He had not told Louis he had proof of the affair on videotape. Why had he taken the pictures of them arriving at the Avalon Motel outside Winona and disappearing into the same unit? He had several other episodes on the same cassette. Call it a hunch, call it intuition. He would never have mentioned those films to Louis. If the doctor was put out by an anonymous phone call what would he make of police surveillance of private citizens?

More food for thought, that phone call. Who had it been? Not that Oscar thought the affair was a secret, certainly not. Several of his own men knew of it, and just in the normal course of events others would have noticed things, put two and two together. He had heard rumors that a Minneapolis private detective had once tailed the couple, but that had been years ago. When he tried to check it out, he drew a blank. The man was dead and if he had kept records no one knew where they were. After the anonymous phone call, Oscar regretted even more that he had been unable to discover who was so interested, to the point of hiring a private investigator, in what Stella and Roy were up to.

The obvious candidate was George Arthur himself, but it strained credulity to think he would not have acted if he had known. His single-minded drive to succeed doubtless blinded George to his domestic situation. There were no children. Oscar looked at Bessie but the Labrador had no explanation for that.

When the maid, Maria Elena, answered the phone, Oscar thought for a moment it was the voice of the anonymous caller. But her accent could not have been sufficiently concealed. He was surer of that after going by the Arthur house and talking with her. A short woman who looked as if she weighed eighty pounds wringing wet from her swim across the Rio Grande, she was as frightened of Oscar as she was of the fact that her employer had not been home for two days.

"Never been away before?"

"She always tell me."

"You're worried?"

She was worried. It was hard to say whether she should be. But her concern gave Oscar an excuse to nose around a bit, and in the course of his nosing he had managed to antagonize Rosemary and Beatrice. Well, why not? Maybe Louis Poeglin was still mad at him too.

On the day after he tried to take an uninvited tour of the silo, Sheriff Ewbank drove out to Lake Owatonna. No reason in particular, he just wanted to revisit the scene of the crime. He could use that phrase talking to Bessie, but would not have said it aloud. That there was reason to think Stella and her lover had done George Arthur in was true enough, but this was Fairland, Minnesota, where murders when they occurred involved no mystery whatsoever, the killer standing over the body with a smoking gun or turning himself in, expecting nothing but punishment. Guesses, motives, circumstantial evidence—these carried no weight in Olson County.

After circling the lake, Ewbank turned in at Roy Hunt's cabin. No sign of anyone around despite the weather. Bessie had hung her head out the window as soon as they arrived at the lake, and when the sheriff pushed open his door after parking behind Hunt's cabin, the Labrador slipped out and went bounding around the corner toward the lake. Oh, to hell with it. Let her have a swim.

Oscar had never learned to swim, not least because he had not cared to expose his body for others to laugh at, but today he would have risked it if he had the time, if he had any right to be at the cabin.

He went around to the front and saw Bessie's head above the water as she swam out from the dock. Oscar went down the hill and out onto the dock, his boots echoing on the separated boards. From somewhere out of sight there came the whine of an outboard and voices carrying over the water. Bessie turned and started back, her eyes rolling with pleasure. Oscar leaned against a post, watching his dog, thinking of George. How many others had drowned in this lake over the years? The first dead man Oscar had ever seen was a fifty-year-old Minneapolitan who was pulled out of the water, blue and dead, ringed by other pop-eyed boys like Oscar. Life and death went on.

Bessie came out of the water and shook herself vigorously before galloping up toward the cabin. Eight years old, Bessie at times thought she was still a puppy and this was one of them. Oscar stayed on the dock, enjoying the cool breeze, the smell of pines, the sense of apartness Lake Owatonna gave. From behind the cabin, Bessie began to set off a racket.

Having swum, she must want to hunt. Oscar wondered what animal she had come upon that made her bark in that excited, frightened way. Reluctantly, he puffed his way up to the cabin. Bessie's barking had turned into a half-frantic yelp and Oscar went around back to investigate.

Bessie's rear was in the air, she was crouched, her muzzle pointed at the door of the tornado cellar dug into the hill. Her eyes rolled up at him as he approached. Had some creature somehow sought refuge in the cellar? Oscar saw no way anything could get in or out the way the door was closed.

It was a garage-type pull-up door. Oscar spread his legs and bent his knees and managed to get a grip on the handle. Easy now. If it was locked and he gave it a hard pull, his back could go out on him.

But the door slid up easily.

The body lay as if it had been pushed and fallen forward into the dank dark interior, a bar of sun slanting in and falling on bare legs. Bessie's barking became hysterical at the sight of the body, and Oscar grabbed her collar to calm her. Part of the face was visible from where he now stood.

Stella Arthur.

TWENTY-ONE

WHAT THE Fairland *Tribune* dubbed the execution-style killing of Stella Arthur, widow of the late George Arthur, provided all the mystery Sheriff Oscar Ewbank or anyone else—well, almost anyone else; the killer of course knew how it had been done—could desire.

Stella had been killed in the tornado shelter, lying where she had fallen, struck from behind, one blow on the crown of the head, another on the back, as if a second had been delivered as she fell away from the first. The weapons proved to be a croquet mallet and the starter rope for an outboard motor, which was twisted around her throat, apparently after she had been rendered unconscious by the blows. The *Tribune* made much of the fact that the weapons were those the location happened to provide and inferred from this that the killing had been unpremeditated, the result of some passion of the moment. Mr. Roy Hunt, president of the First Southeastern Bank of Fairland, on whose property the body had been found, refused to speak to the *Tribune*.

Roy had been rendered speechless by the sight of the body and all the anger he had felt as he brooded over Oscar Ewbank's mystifying call during the drive to the lake had evaporated.

"I'm at your place on Lake Owatonna," Oscar had said. "Could you come right out here?"

"What's wrong?"

"Another body has washed up on your shore, Roy."

"What the hell does that mean?"

But the sheriff had hung up. Roy dialed the number of the cabin and got a busy signal. The image of Oscar Ewbank occupying his cabin and making phone calls galore brought him to his feet. How the hell had Oscar got in? Roy would have called the police except that Oscar was the police, so far as Fairland was concerned. Oscar had been the police too long, that's what the problem was, the sheriff's office being treated as a hereditary fiefdom of the Ewbank family. The strutting comic figure of the sheriff, that stupid phone call, the fact that he was responding to it and dutifully driving to the lake, all enraged Roy Hunt.

Another body washed up on your shore! Some poor devil drowned and Oscar had to justify his existence by giving owners of lakefront property a hard time. Roy would bet it had been a water-skiing accident. The way those young fools skimmed across the water, zigging and zagging and doing everything else to increase the hazard of the ride, it was a wonder they didn't all break their necks.

The farther he got from town, the more he felt the pull of the work he was leaving behind. Taking this kind of unscheduled recess from his duties at the bank was something he had always been willing to do when Stella called. They had to take their opportunities as they came. But for that jackass Oscar Ewbank to screw up his day like this called for a chewing-out that would let Oscar know precisely where he stood in the Fairland pecking order.

Roy Hunt had been the unsuccessful candidate in the election for senior class president, losing to Oscar Ewbank! It was bad enough to lose, but to lose to a clown like Ewbank made it worse. When had people started taking Oscar seriously? Sooner than Roy, apparently. He had considered the election a mere formality, a public endorsement of his class leadership. For a week, he had been practicing the offhand remarks he would make when the results were announced.

And he had lost. Almost against his will, Roy had followed Oscar's subsequent career. He rejoiced, he admitted it to himself and to Stella, when Oscar's bright prospects turned into nothing more than being sheriff of Olson County. Oscar might have had undiscovered talent, but he sure as hell didn't have ambition.

The three patrol cars standing in the driveway to the cabin were more than he expected, but his wrath did not diminish as he pulled in, got out of his car, and slammed the door. What the hell were all those people doing by his storm shelter? Oscar Ewbank, drawn by the slamming door, waddled toward Roy, the Goodyear blimp in dress uniform.

"What's going on?"

Oscar took his elbow. "I wanted you to see this, Roy."

The deference in the sheriff's voice disarmed Roy. Besides, he was curious now to see what all those deputies were doing at the shelter. They stepped aside for Oscar.

What Roy first saw was Dr. Lindquist kneeling on the dirt floor, a handkerchief spread to protect his light blue trousers. And then he realized that the body Lindquist was looking at was Stella's.

Oscar was gripping his arm, but Roy pulled free and dropped to the ground beside Lindquist, looking wildly from the doctor to Stella. Then he saw the wooden handle of the outboard motor starter, the rope coming through the hole and then its tufted ends knotted. At the moment, Roy felt he could see each strand in the rope, and grain in the wood of the handle where the red paint had been worn away. He reached forward to get the damned thing off Stella's throat, but Lindquist said, "Better not touch it, Roy."

All he could think was that the rope was hurting Stella. After that, things got a bit blurred and confused. It took three deputies to pull Roy out of the shelter and into the cabin, where they pushed him into a chair.

"You want a drink, Roy? I think you need a drink."

Oscar told one of the deputies there was some bourbon in the kitchen cabinet. How the hell did he know that? Roy wouldn't have remembered the bottle. But he had lost all authority in his own cabin. He took the bourbon and tossed it off without effect. He closed his eyes, then opened them again because the image of Stella's body formed inside his lids. Lindquist came in and a medical examiner from the state police, who said she had been dead at least twenty-four hours, at most forty-eight.

"She's been missing for two days," Oscar said.

Roy followed this now from a psychological distance, far enough away not to be hurt by what he heard, yet near enough to understand. What did they mean by saying Stella had been missing for two days?

The two of them had spent the night before last right here in the cabin. He had left first, he had to get to the office, but Stella was already up when he left. She would follow a little later, as she always had.

The medical examiner was reciting things aloud as he entered them onto a clipboard. He described the wounds, the signs of strangulation, the estimated time of death. Lindquist nodded through it all. They might have been two pilots checking out a plane before takeoff. They were talking of Stella. It was unreal. The room cleared after a while and there was only Oscar left.

"Feeling better, Roy?"

"This has been a shock."

"That's why I said as little as I did on the phone. So what do you think?"

"What do I think?"

Oscar waited, as if embarrassed. "Why here?"

"I don't know what you mean."

"Why was Stella killed here at your cabin, Roy? Did you know she was here?"

"No. She could come here if she wanted, of course, but why today..."

"She hadn't been staying here?"

Careful, careful. Oscar had known about the bourbon in the kitchen. What else did he know? Maybe Stella hadn't made the bed and cleaned up before leaving. All he had to do was ask the question to know the answer.

"Not to my knowledge."

"The bed had been slept in."

"Perhaps she had used the place."

"She had a key?"

"She knew where I hid it."

"Where would that be?"

"The sill over the back door."

"Show me."

When Roy stood up he felt dizzy, perhaps from the whiskey. Oscar made as if to help him, but Roy steadied himself and walked through the kitchen. He let Oscar out, let the screen door slam, then felt above the door. He found the key.

"This is it."

"So she didn't use it."

"Why do you say that?"

"The door was unlocked."

"She could have put the key back after unlocking the door."

Oscar said nothing, pulled open the screen door, and gestured Roy inside.

"Look, I should be getting back to my office," Roy said. He glanced toward the shelter. The door was shut, the area was staked off, a deputy stood some twenty yards off smoking a cigarette with great concentration.

"I have to ask you a few more questions."

Roy bristled at the implication. "Oscar, if you think I know anything about what happened to Stella, forget it." But he went inside, telling himself to take it easy. If he were Oscar he would want to put a few questions himself.

"This has been a shock," he said, seated again. How many times had he said that?

"You want more of that bourbon?"

He shook his head.

"Mind if I do?"

"Go ahead. Maybe I will have a little." It wouldn't hurt to get things on a better footing. Both he and Oscar had known Stella. But no one had known Stella as he had. Roy looked out at the lake, his eyes flooding with tears.

"First George, now Stella," Oscar sighed, handing Roy a glass. He then settled into a chair with a very dark-looking bourbon and water in his own hand. "And both at Lake Owatonna."

Roy burst into tears, surprising himself. He sat there holding his weak drink in one hand, looking with tear-blurred eyes across the room to where the lake was vaguely visible through the windows, blubbering like a kid. But he felt like a kid, to hell with the fact that he was forty years old. Losing Stella was like losing part of himself.

"You were pretty close," Oscar said when Roy's sobbing had run its course and subsided.

The question brought Roy back into the room. Stella was not only dead, she had been strangled. Killed. Murdered. The sheriff was going to have to find the one who did it. And Roy Hunt meant to give him all the help he could.

"I can't imagine who could have done this, Oscar."

Oscar ran a fat finger around the brim of the cowboy hat he had put on the couch beside him.

"I got a funny phone call about you and Stella not long ago, Roy."

"I suppose you get a lot of funny phone calls."

"Not like this one. The caller wanted me to believe that you and Stella had something to do with George Arthur's death."

"We did. I took him ice fishing. He'd be alive today if I hadn't."

"I think that was the caller's point."

Killing George had been so long ago, retaining a dreamlike reality at best, that Roy was not immediately wary. Who could regard Oscar Ewbank as a menacing figure?

"The caller said that you and Stella were a lot more than friends, that you met regularly in various places, that you were lovers."

"No wonder the call was anonymous."

"Did I say that?"

"Wasn't it?"

"I'm more interested in the message. Is it true, Roy?"

From this point in the conversation, Roy knew that a combination of factors would indeed make Oscar inquire into any possibility that he had killed Stella. That he himself found that possibility impossible would not be good enough for Oscar. And so he answered with care.

"Stella and I have been friends since high school, Oscar. We went together as kids."

"I remember. But you never married."

"Neither have you."

"But I had no chance with girls like Stella."

"There were no girls like Stella."

"So you went on loving her?"

"I suppose."

"Even after she was married?"

"I don't drop my friends when they marry, Oscar. Do you?"

"How many other old married friends do you screw every week or so?"

The question was meant to enrage him and of course it did. He got to his feet as if he meant to whip Oscar. Then he looked down at the pathetic bulk of the sheriff and shook his head.

"I'm going back to my office."

Oscar shook his head too. "No, Roy. I'd rather not arrest you formally but I will. I have more questions."

"If you put it on that basis, I want a lawyer present."

Oscar pushed forward, put one hand on the back of the couch, the other on the cushion beside him, gripped the brim of his hat, and then in a heaving, rolling motion got himself standing. His expression was almost triumphant.

"I was just going to suggest that."

"You sonofabitch."

"Why don't you call your lawyer?"

AXEL LUND hummed along as he listened to what Roy had to say, then suggested that he come out to the lake. "Better there than in my office or at the courthouse."

The courthouse! While they waited for Axel to come, Roy sat on the porch looking out over Lake Owatonna. All his life he had been familiar with that scene. He had learned to fish and sail on that lake, he had learned to swim in it. From the end of May until after Labor Day this had been where the Hunt family lived. His father came out only on weekends, but it was as if he were away rather than the family. So vivid were these memories that Roy half expected to hear his mother calling him to the table. The clouds overhead reminded him of sudden storms. It was his mother's fear of storms at the lake, when the pines would bend and bow, that had prompted the digging of the tornado shelter. Roy could remember cowering in that dank shelter with his mother, waiting for the rain to end. A place designed for shelter and safety had proven fatal to Stella.

Who killed her? It seemed clear that she had never left the place two days before. Someone had come to the cabin and killed her. Roy's mind formed the figure of a man, a faceless silhouette, accompanied by an unwelcome thought. Had the man come because Stella had asked him? Jealousy swept over him. While George was alive, Roy had felt no jealousy. He had never doubted Stella when she said she felt nothing for her husband. But since George's death, Roy had felt on more than one occasion the twinge of jealousy. It did not help to know, as he did, that Stella would do anything that pleased her.

Oscar brought Axel out to the porch and Roy stood to shake hands with his lawyer. Lund was tall, cadaverous, blue-eyed, and stoop-shouldered. He cast a birdlike glance on Oscar.

"You were asking Roy some questions, I believe. Why don't you go on? Until I stop you, that is." His teeth were revealed slowly as his lips formed a smile.

"Axel, the sheriff got a call telling him that Stella and I were lovers. Naturally this makes him think I must have killed her."

"Did you?" Axel asked.

"No."

Lund looked at the sheriff. "Now you know what you wanted to know."

Oscar had not taken his eyes from Roy. "Did Stella stay here with you two nights ago, Roy?"

Lund was as interested in the answer as Oscar. Roy nodded.

"Tell me about that morning."

"I got up, washed, put on coffee, drove to town. It was a business day."

"Was Stella up when you left?"

"I brought her a cup of coffee. We said goodbye." He stopped. How could he have known that goodbye was goodbye indeed?

"Did you return here that night?"

"No. I stayed in town."

"So your night here was just that, a one-nighter?"

"Oscar, it's none of your goddamn business, but, yes, Stella and I were more than friends."

"And had been for years?"

"Yes."

"And you and Stella were together with her husband when he died in the lake."

"Whoa," Lund intervened. "It is a matter of record that George Arthur died by accidental drowning while ice fishing. The only relevance his death has to the matter at hand is that it makes it far less surprising that Stella should have spent the night with Roy."

"It was a weekly event, Axel. It had been for years."

"Let's talk about Stella's death, shall we, Oscar?"

"All right. Roy and Stella had a public fight at the country club just two days before Stella was killed."

"Are you suggesting a falling-out?"

"That's right."

"Over what?"

"Money."

Axel stopped Oscar definitively then, scoffed at the suggestion that Roy was under arrest, assured the sheriff that his client would always be available for the forces of law and order. Lund waited until Oscar had finally driven away, leaving one deputy still posted by the staked-off storm shelter.

"A hell of a note," Axel said. "Is there any beer here?"

He did not dawdle over the beer, but drank it standing, in long drafts, his eyes seldom leaving Roy.

"Weren't you and Oscar in the same class, Roy?"

"With Stella."

"What else has he got against you?"

"She did spend the night here, Axel. We never stopped loving one another, Stella and I."

"And George?"

"He bought her father's business. It was her way of hanging on to it."

"It's easy to see how Oscar's mind will work, Roy. If she married the man only to keep possession of the business, she might have killed him in order to have it all."

"I don't see why we have to keep talking about George. It's Stella who's been killed."

"But Oscar will imagine both of them were, and then he is going to see you as next in line."

"To be killed?"

"No."

"Axel, come on. Why would I kill Stella?"

"Why did you fight with her in front of everyone at the country club?"

Eventually he would see that there was no way to avoid answering such questions, at least when they were put by his lawyer. Eventually he told Axel everything, well, almost everything. Maybe Axel suspected that he and Stella had killed George, but Roy wasn't going to say it. He could say what he needed to say on the assumption that George's death had been an accident.

George Arthur sounded like a real eccentric when you thought of all that cash around his house, and Axel nodded agreement when Roy recounted his efforts to get George to put his money in the bank.

"Why a safe-deposit box?"

"George considered this nontaxable money."

"Ah."

"He would have paid a lot more in taxes than he would have earned in interest."

"How much money?"

"Seven hundred and fifty thousand."

"Well, well."

"I saw him put it in there."

"I believe you, Roy." Lund must have thought then of all that secret money and its owner dead. "Is it still there?"

"No."

This was the hard part, explaining to Axel about the empty box.

"You opened it, Roy?"

"With Stella. It was hers too. She had one of the keys."

"And George had the other?"

"That's right."

"So who opened the box?"

"We figured it was George."

"Roy, how's he going to do that without you being there. Anyone else know which box was the secret one?"

Roy looked open mouthed at Axel.

"Couldn't be done, could it, Roy? And Stella couldn't do it either. Not without your help."

Axel Lund was absolutely right. Roy took comfort from the confusion on his lawyer's face. Maybe now the sonofabitch could understand how Roy felt.

"There's something else, Axel. Another possibility."

"Another? So far we've got impossibilities."

Roy explained to Axel about the sale of George's books, of Stella's suspicion that George's copy of the key had gone to Steve Nicodemus, the bookseller, and that Nicodemus had somehow gotten Phyllis's help in opening the box and removing the money. Axel's eyebrows lifted in disbelief.

"Roy, that's dumb. Why would Phyllis do a thing like that?"

"I don't know! You have to talk to her."

Axel shook his head. "But she didn't know which box was the secret one, did she?"

Roy sat back. "You see why this is driving me crazy, Axel. It couldn't be done, yet somehow someone did it. And it could have been Nicodemus. I found George's key hidden in Nicodemus's box."

Axel listened to the explanation of that, his head swaying back and forth.

"What a tangled web this is, Roy."

The upshot of their conversation was that Axel advised Roy to tell Oscar Ewbank about the safe-deposit box, the missing key, and the dubious book dealer.

"But it's against regulations to rent a box blind like that."

"Let us hope that will prove to be your greatest difficulty, Roy."

And so it was that Roy Hunt told a skeptical Oscar Ewbank about the missing key to George Arthur's safe-deposit box, in the hope of deflecting the sheriff's attention to Steve Nicodemus.

TWENTY-TWO

As SHERIFF of Olson County, Oscar Ewbank had met at least half a dozen killers but never once what he would have called a murderer. Killers use knives or guns in a moment of passion, their victims are relatives, usually a spouse, or at least a lover. But a murderer sets out to end another person's life, plans it, executes the plan, hopes to evade suspicion and profit from what he has done. If George Arthur's death was not accidental, he had been murdered. The case of Stella was less clear, but it looked like murder to Oscar Ewbank. And Oscar Ewbank was determined to apprehend his first murderer.

It seemed obvious that Roy Hunt was his quarry. And that made it ridiculous to think Roy himself was next on the putative murderer's hit list. Oscar held himself responsible for introducing this particular fancy. Roy was understandably eager to turn attention away from himself by suggesting that the bookseller Nicodemus, or George Arthur's administrative assistant Beatrice, was responsible for Stella's death— and, if it wasn't an accident, for George's too.

"Why not you too then?" Oscar asked Roy.

"You're right! I'm probably next."

Lund liked that. "I want special protection for my client, Oscar."

Oscar nodded, but not in agreement. Special protection. He had only a dozen deputies and six of those

worked out of their homes in various parts of the
county. Three on, three off, in Fairland, how was he
supposed to provide a bodyguard for Roy Hunt?

"I live in fear, Oscar."

He seemed to mean it. "We'll see."

"Yes or no?" Lund demanded.

He promised to talk to Nicodemus and Beatrice,
which cheered Roy up, but Axel would not drop the
demand that Oscar provide round-the-clock protection for Roy as a constitutional right.

"He can stay here in jail."

Lund blew up and so did Oscar, in his way. He demanded to see the vault in Roy's bank where the safe-
deposit boxes were.

"What in the world for?" Lund asked, placing his
hand on Roy's arm. His client had not yet acquired the
habit of letting his lawyer speak for him.

"It seems to play a big part in Roy's story."

"Only in a negative way, Oscar. Roy mentioned an
empty box. Do you want to waste time examining an
empty box or do you want to follow up on the leads
you've been given?"

"Axel, do I tell you how to do your job?"

"I'm always open to suggestions."

"Then let's go to the bank."

"As soon as you talk with your two suspects."

"Suspects! Axel, your client is my suspect."

Lund thought a moment. "One of your suspects,
I'll grant you that. Let's compromise. You round up
the others and we'll *all* go to the bank."

Oscar accepted, if only because Roy Hunt obviously didn't like it. He did insist on one proviso.

"In the meantime, Roy'll have to stay here."

Axel had to wrestle Roy back into his chair. He looked at Oscar over his shoulder.

"That's not necessary, Oscar."

"Oh yes it is. Unless you want to go to the bank now."

"What is this fixation with the bank?"

"Roy is the one who mentioned the safe-deposit box."

"Get the other suspects, Oscar."

"Arrest them," Roy said. "If I'm arrested, arrest them too."

"If I find a body on their property, I'll do that."

Oscar ignored the obscenity Roy spat at him. This was like a continuation of their high school rivalry. Oscar had beaten Roy then and he beat him now, leaving him not in a cell but in an office, with Chuck Wagner, a deputy, on guard outside the door.

OSCAR KNEW the road on which Nicodemus both lived and conducted his business, but only twice before had he turned into the drive and come to a stop on the apron in front of the garage. He switched off the engine and sat behind the wheel. It was an old trick, not to make the first move, just show the flag and see what happened next. What happened next was nothing.

The water in the pool glistened in the sun, towels hung heavy and damp on a line stretched from the house to an elm; the door of the house did not open nor did Oscar detect anyone taking a peek out the window. He pushed open the door of the car and eased his belly out from under the wheel. Bessie was content to stay in back so Oscar left her, cracking the windows so she would have plenty of air.

A sheriff's car with a big shield on the door and a light mounted on top and now the sheriff himself in full panoply of office, and still nothing happened. Oscar sauntered down the walk that led past the garage to the door of the bookstore. OPEN. He pushed on the door and set off a jangle of bells, but did not himself go in. If that didn't get a response he would know Nicodemus was playing possum.

"Can I help you?"

Oscar had not heard her come up behind him and he jumped at the sound of her voice. Why the hell hadn't Bessie warned him?

"Mrs. Nicodemus?"

"Are you the sheriff or just a deputy?"

He took off his cap. "Oscar Ewbank, ma'am. Sheriff of Olson County."

"Steve's not here."

"I'd hoped to talk with him."

"I expect him any minute. Would you like coffee?"

"If it's made."

She took his elbow and led him back up the walk and then over to the picnic table.

"I'll be back in a jiff."

She brought the coffee in mugs and Oscar sipped his looking over the pool toward the trees at the end of the property.

"What's on the other side of that wood?"

"The country club. Tell me about Stella Arthur."

"Did you know her?"

"In a business way. We bought her husband's books. She wasn't easy to do business with."

"How so?"

"After she sold the books, she thought she wanted them back but she couldn't make up her mind."

"Why would she have wanted them back?"

"Search me." She smiled. "Maybe I shouldn't say that to a sheriff."

"Your husband ever say why he thought she wanted them back?"

"Here's Steve now."

She pointed to the van that had pulled to a stop next to Oscar's car. Bessie decided to object to that. Her barking brought Mrs. Nicodemus to her feet.

"Let the dog out, sheriff. He can't get into any trouble here."

Oscar's eyes were on the bald, bearded man who came toward them as if his belly were a bass drum he was carrying. Oscar was trying to see him as if for the first time.

"Let her out if you want to," Oscar said to the woman. "Her name's Bessie."

"Bessie!" Off she went to Oscar's car.

Nicodemus put out his hand. "She's always wanted a dog."

"Can we talk?"

"How about in the store?"

Over Mrs. Nicodemus's objections, as it turned out. Bessie wasn't sufficient to deflect her interest from Stella Arthur and she wanted to know what the latest was.

"The autopsy report isn't available yet."

"Who did it? Who killed her?"

"That's what we're trying to find out."

It seemed not to have occurred to her that his visit here had anything to do with Stella's death, even though she had been quick to mention buying George Arthur's books. All in all, a disarming reaction. Nicodemus hadn't said anything. Now, more or less ignoring his wife's curiosity, he led the way to the bookstore. Oscar followed, bringing his mug of coffee along.

"You did business with Stella Arthur?"

"I bought her husband's books."

"Your wife said she had trouble making up her mind about that."

"She thought they were worth more than they were. People often do. When she realized my offer was fair, she sold them. Later she talked about buying them back."

"Why?"

"I don't know."

Oscar looked around. "How many books you got here?"

"Guess."

"I haven't a clue."

"Thirty-five thousand, more or less."

"How many did George Arthur have?"

"Four thousand. He had a very handsome library. She wanted to sell me the shelving too, but I had no use for it. Her niece took the shelving."

"You heard what happened to her?"

"To Stella Arthur? Of course. I read the paper."

"I've been questioning Roy Hunt."

Nicodemus nodded.

"Do you know anything about a safe-deposit key?"

"One connected with the Arthurs?"

"Yes."

"A safe deposit key fell out of one of the books I bought from her."

"What did you do with it?"

"I returned it to her, of course."

They went over it several times, how the red envelope had fallen out of the book, how Nicodemus recognized what it was because he had such a key himself.

He took an envelope out of the desk drawer and handed it to Oscar. "This is exactly like the one that was in the book. The same bank."

Oscar took the red envelope, unsnapped it, and let the key slide into the palm of his hand.

"What's it to?"

"My safe-deposit box, obviously."

"How long did you have the Arthur key?"

"After I found it? A week. Maybe more."

"Did it fit?"

Nicodemus might have been counting to ten. "I hope you're not suggesting that I tried to use it."

"Did you?"

"Of course not."

"Why did you keep it so long?"

"I offered it to Mrs. Arthur, but at first she didn't want it."

"You took it to her?"

"She came here."

"When was that?"

Nicodemus looked at the ceiling. "Today's what, Friday? I think it was Monday."

"You saw her on Monday?"

"She was here in the store, yes."

"On Monday. Did you see her after that?"

"No."

"Why didn't she want the key?"

"She didn't say."

"I'm told there was a great deal of money in the box that key opens. Money that's no longer there."

"Maybe that's why she didn't want the key."

"Where is the key now?"

"I mailed it. She wouldn't take it, so I put it in the mail."

Like many quiet places, the bookstore proved to have its own sounds: the steady whirr of the air conditioner, the ticking of the clock, a thud on the back wall, maybe the metal buckling. The cat was soundless. Oscar didn't want Bessie to see that cat.

"Did she mention any missing money?"

"Money hidden in the books?"

"Money in a safe-deposit box."

"Why would she tell me such a thing?"

"Because you had the key for at least a week."

"Sheriff, do you have a safe-deposit box?"

"No."

"If you found that key of mine, do you think you could open my box? As a private citizen?"

"I don't know."

"You couldn't."

"You sound as if you tried."

"Even if I had wanted to, it couldn't be done."

"Would you be willing to come down to the bank, Mr. Nicodemus?"

"To the bank! What for?"

"I want Roy Hunt to open that box."

"It's his bank."

"He's also under suspicion in the murder of Stella Arthur."

"Why do you want me there?"

"I need witnesses. You're a registered voter, aren't you?"

It worked. But maybe Nicodemus was more curious than deceived. And mentioning that Beatrice Dean would be there too didn't hurt.

"I'll come by for you, Mr. Nicodemus, after I talk with Miss Dean."

WHEN OSCAR was shown into her office, Beatrice Dean waited for him to cross to her desk. She did not ask him to sit down.

"I've arrested Roy Hunt."

She said nothing, just looked up at him. A tough cookie.

"For the death of Stella Arthur."

A slight nod.

"I understand you didn't get along with Mrs. Arthur."

"What do you want, sheriff?"

"I would like you to be there when Roy Hunt shows me a safe-deposit box from which he says a great deal of money is missing."

"Why?"

"As a witness."

She thought about it, her head tilted as if she were listening to advice. "All right."

He couldn't believe it. He was feeling like a kid called before the principal, sure he was on a wild-goose chase. Why the hell should she agree to come down to the bank to witness the opening of a safe-deposit box? But she agreed. You'd think she had expected this unlikely scenario.

"When?"

"As soon as possible."

"I'll be there in half an hour."

On the way back to pick up Nicodemus, he puzzled over the ease with which he had accomplished his fool's errand. Bessie sat in the back, happy and wet from her unscheduled swim in the Nicodemus pool.

THE WAY Phyllis's lower lip was tucked under her teeth she had the look of someone about to say Shame! Or about to cry. Probably cry, and who could blame her, the way Roy Hunt treated her? The woman was flustered when they all arrived at her post—Roy, Axel Lund, Beatrice Dean, Nicodemus, Oscar, and Chuck Wagner. Roy finally snatched the ring of keys from her and led them into the vault.

Oscar was reminded of the mausoleum in which he had buried his father, walls lined with boxes, even the smell. They gathered around a chest-high table in the center of the room and Axel asked Roy to explain the procedure so everyone would be clear about it. Only Chuck and Axel listened closely to what Roy was saying. Beatrice might have been meditating. Nicodemus stood with folded arms, staring at the ceiling.

"George Arthur wanted an unregistered box here. I agreed. Foolishly, no doubt, but I agreed. I witnessed him put seven hundred and fifty thousand dollars into that box. After his death, I witnessed his wife open that box and find it empty."

"An unregistered box?" Beatrice asked.

"That's right."

"How would anyone know whose it was then?"

"I knew. George Arthur knew."

"And Stella," Oscar said.

Oscar said, "Open the box, Roy."

Roy placed the little stepladder, climbed it, and inserted a key from the ring he had taken from Phyllis into one of the slots. He then produced another key and began to put it in the second slot.

Beatrice said, "Where did that key come from?"

"From Stella Arthur."

"What are you doing with it?"

There was silence in the vault. Roy, perched unsteadily on the ladder, looked at the faces below. "I was with Mrs. Arthur when she opened this box before," he said steadily.

"And you kept the key?"

"She left it with me. The box was empty. I suppose she felt the key was useless."

He turned away from them and twisted the two keys, lifted the little door, and slid out a long green metal box. When it was free of the compartment, Roy nearly lost his balance and Chuck Wagner stepped forward to take the green box.

"Put it on the table, Chuck," Oscar said.

Roy scampered down the ladder and pushed his way up to the table, taking possession of the box, a puzzled expression on his face. He undid a little fastener and opened the hinged lid.

"Good God!"

The box was completely filled with neat packages of bills of large denominations.

ROY HUNT unraveled. He had been under pressure since arriving at the cabin at Lake Owatonna. Stella's body had brought on a strange reaction, bereaved lover or guilty killer, who could say? The back-and-forth with Axel Lund getting in his two cents' worth had made the pressure mount. Roy had mentioned the box, it was at the heart of his story, it was Axel who hadn't wanted to come to the bank. Roy was willing enough. The box was what would turn attention away from him. Seeing it chock-full of money knocked him for a loop. He babbled. He lost all sense of caution. Despite the crowded room, Oscar pressed his advantage, with Axel desperately trying to shut his client up. Oscar got him out of the vault and made a sandwich of him on the backseat of Chuck's cruiser—Lund on one side, Oscar on the other, the babbling banker in the middle.

"You spent Monday night in your cabin on Lake Owatonna with Stella, didn't you, Roy?"

"Don't answer that, Roy."

"Yes."

"And you publicly fought with her before that at the country club, right?"

"Roy..."

"That money was gone, I swear it was. The box was empty."

"You spent Tuesday and Wednesday nights at the lake with Stella."

"We checked the box together. I thought Stella..."

Axel was beside himself. "Roy, will you shut your goddamn mouth."

"On Wednesday you killed her. You struck her on the head with a mallet and then you twisted that rope around her neck..."

Roy began to shake his head. "No, no."

"Good, Roy," Axel said. "Good. That's all you've got to say."

"It was George," Roy went on. "We killed George and what the hell for? We pushed him through the ice and slammed the door..."

"You killed George Arthur?"

"Oscar, this is useless." Axel cupped both his knees in his large hands. "No judge in the country would admit the confession of a man clearly in shock."

But Roy seemed relieved to have said it and he went on talking. Maybe it made sense that even in this confessional mood he waved off Oscar's efforts to get him to admit killing Stella. He kept coming back to the money in the box.

"Maybe Stella didn't take it out, Roy."

"Maybe she put it back. First, she took it out, then she put it back. But why?"

"So you killed her for nothing."

"We killed George for nothing."

"God," Axel groaned, throwing up his hands.

TWENTY-THREE

ROSEMARY WAS in Minneapolis the afternoon the money was found in the unregistered safe-deposit box, and when she returned she got the story from Beatrice.

"Whose box was it?"

"Roy Hunt says it was George's."

"Was it?"

"It wasn't registered."

"But why would Roy have made such a big production of it?"

"Guilt?"

The money was no longer in the freezer. Rosemary stacked meat up on the dryer until she reached the bottom of the freezer chest. No money.

Had she really seen a layer of packaged money beneath all that frozen meat? She tried to come up with other memories of that day and they were vague. What remained vivid was removing packages of meat and discovering all those other packages beneath. She hadn't dreamed that. And now the money was gone. It was hard not to connect it with the money that had reappeared in the safe-deposit box.

"Who does the money belong to, Beatrice?"

"You, I suppose."

"Me!"

"Aren't you the heir?"

"Is it the same money that was in the freezer?"

Beatrice turned and looked directly at her. A moment of silence went by. "There is also money in a safe-deposit box George asked me to rent in my name."

Just like that.

"It will all be yours now, the money George had hidden away. We were going to live on that money, George and I." Beatrice's eyes drifted to the window, seeking some impossible horizon over which she and George would have disappeared to live happily ever after. Sadness swept over her face like the shadow of clouds. Rosemary's heart went out to Beatrice. Whatever happiness she had planned with George would never be. Once more, they were birds of a feather.

STEVE NICODEMUS, when Rosemary stopped by the bookstore, no longer reminded her of Russ. She realized it made him uneasy to talk about Stella and what had happened to her and her husband. But he didn't find it strange that Roy should admit to killing George and deny killing Stella.

"They'd been friends since they were kids."

"Friends."

He seemed embarrassed. She asked him about the key.

"When it fell out of the book, I remembered your mentioning money hidden in your uncle's books. Your aunt wouldn't take the key when I tried to give it to her. Now I understand why."

"I don't."

"The box it opened was supposed to contain money. She had found it empty. I suppose she thought I was responsible."

"So you mailed it to her?"

He ran a finger from the tip of his nose, through his mustache, over his lips, and down through his beard to his chest. "I mailed it to its owner, George Arthur."

"So she would have got it."

"If she picked up his mail at the office."

"You sent it to his office?"

"That's right."

If Beatrice received it, that explained how she had been able to put the money back into the box. It seemed an expensive way to trap the ones who had killed the man she loved, but then, the money didn't belong to Beatrice anyway. It made Rosemary a little dizzy to think of all that money as her own.

When they left the bookstore, Mrs. Nicodemus and Babs Poeglin were having coffee near the pool and Rosemary and the bookseller joined them.

"You didn't sell her any books," Mrs. Nicodemus complained to her husband.

"Maybe I'll buy back my uncle's books."

Nicodemus groaned. "Now you tell me."

"Are they scattered all over?"

"I could get them all together. Are you serious?"

Rosemary imagined the house restored to the way it had been before these tragic events. Thank God she still had the bookshelves. She told Nicodemus she was serious.

"Will you be living in the house?" Babs Poeglin asked.

Rosemary thought about it. Move to Fairland, manage her inherited wealth? Of course, Beatrice would stay on.

"It looks like it."

Babs shook her head. "There's a whole world out there and you want to live in Fairland?" What depths of discontent sounded in her voice.

Rosemary was still there when Dr. Poeglin arrived. He came from his parked car almost at a jog and sat on a bench of the picnic table, his eyes on everyone but his wife.

"What a terrible thing," he said to Rosemary.

She accepted the sentiment, not quite knowing what to do. It seemed hypocritical to pretend she had been closer to Stella and George than she was.

"If I hadn't been in surgery, I might have been able to help. Perhaps not, but I like to think so."

"Stella was Louis's patient," Babs explained to the world. She got to her feet and her husband was immediately on his.

"We'll meet at the club," he said. It sounded like an order.

"Poor Babs," Mabel murmured as the Poeglins got into their separate cars and drove away. "He really keeps an eye on her."

"Ever since Minneapolis."

Rosemary wrinkled her nose to indicate incomprehension and Steve told the story of Babs Poeglin and the Erickson auction.

"She thought she wanted excitement until she found it."

"Steve!" Mabel said.

"Didn't she try to lead you astray?"

"That'll be the day."

THE COMPACT woman with severely cut hair who came to the door of the house did not at first identify herself as a Unitarian minister.

"I'm Claudia Cartwright. Please accept my condolences."

Rosemary assumed this was a friend of Stella and George.

"I understand you'll be living in Fairland."

"Well, I don't want to sell this house."

"I don't blame you," she said, having given the living room a sweeping glance.

"I'm drinking coffee," Rosemary said.

"You shouldn't."

"But even breathing is dangerous, isn't it?"

"You mustn't get the wrong impression of this town because of what happened to your aunt and uncle."

"Are you a native?"

"No!" She said too quickly, almost bleating it. "I've been pastor here for over four years."

"Pastor?"

"Of the Unitarian church. I hope you'll come. Babs Poeglin suggested I ask you. You'll find my sermons have to do with the real world, and if I say so, they are particularly relevant to women's concerns."

"I'm not much of a churchgoer."

"Few of my parishioners were."

Rosemary was trying to guess why Babs Poeglin had played this trick on her. She mentioned meeting the Poeglins at the bookstore.

"What did you think of him?"

The question seemed to be the hidden one whose answer would tell all.

"He was only there a minute."

"He oppresses her. He dreads her independence. There are still men like that. I flatter myself that I have something to do with his unease. He forbade Babs's attending my church, but of course I put a stop to that. There is such a thing as freedom of worship. I threatened to sue him."

She folded the arms of her pin-striped suit and smiled with satisfaction at Rosemary.

"Come on Sunday, Rosemary. Give it a try. I think you'll like it."

It seemed a victory not to promise.

PARKER THE prosecutor arraigned Roy on a charge of first-degree murder in the death of George Arthur. There were pro forma delays but the trial took place in November. Axel pleaded his client innocent, but on the stand, Roy made it clear enough to the jury that he and Stella had planned and executed the death of her husband George. The jury returned a verdict of guilty and the judge ordered an examination to determine whether Roy Hunt was of sound mind. He was and had been, although he seemed obsessive on the subject of the safe-deposit box to which he had led the sheriff and which had proved his undoing. Everyone assumed he had killed Stella too. The fact that his lawyer bent his best efforts to place the blame for George's death on Stella and to portray Roy as her unwitting dupe seemed to provide motive for his murdering her.

Roy Hunt's eyes were wide and wary when he came into the visiting room and saw Rosemary. After a moment, he came toward her and the guard, who had stopped inside the door, shifted his weight. Roy sat across from Rosemary.

"I didn't kill Stella," he said earnestly. "I deserve to be here, but not for that."

"Is there anything I can do for you, anything you need?"

His eyes filled with tears. "Thank you."

"I believe you about Stella."

"It's true!"

"Then who did it?"

He looked around, half wildly. "Whoever took that money."

One of the things established in the trial was that there was only Roy Hunt's word that the safe-deposit box had ever been emptied of money.

"But why?"

"Stella must have known." He leaned forward. "I think it was the bookseller, Nicodemus."

Roy sounded crazy, but who could blame him? Rosemary wondered if it was wise to encourage him in the claim that someone else had killed Stella. But she had meant it when she said she believed him. Why would he kill the woman he loved?

She said, "Dr. Poeglin thinks he might have saved Stella if he had been called."

"He was called."

"He meant if he had been able to come."

"It was his day off. Wednesday."

"No. He was in surgery."

"On Wednesday? I doubt it. But it doesn't matter. Nobody could have helped Stella." He shook his head. "What drives me crazy is that safe-deposit box. I know it was empty. Who put the money back?"

It was tempting to ease his mind and tell him it had been Beatrice, but Rosemary said nothing. The net effect of what Beatrice had done was to entrap George's killer. It was hard to see what comfort Roy could derive from knowing that.

LOUIS POEGLIN was at the building site of his new clinic, according to his nurse Miss Mulvaney.

"Is that how he spends his day off?"

Miss Mulvaney smiled. "He'll golf later, but he loves making a pest of himself at the new clinic."

"When will it be finished?"

"Next month. The target is May first."

"How long does it take to build a clinic?"

"They broke ground last August."

"When Stella Arthur was killed."

"Was that in August?"

"August sixteenth. A Wednesday."

Miss Mulvaney smiled, as if waiting for Rosemary to make sense.

"What was Dr. Poeglin doing that day, visiting the site?"

"I suppose."

"Could he have been in surgery?"

"On a Wednesday?" The little starched cap moved like a weathervane as she shook her head. "Never on a Wednesday. That's the theme song of this office."

"Can you check and see?"

Miss Mulvaney frowned. "See what doctor was doing last August sixteenth?"

"Have you ever half remembered a tune and driven yourself nuts trying to recall the words?"

"All the time. I can never remember jokes or lyrics."

She was flipping through the appointment book she had taken from a lower drawer. Her lacquered nail slid down a page. The weathervane turned east and west. "No. It was a normal Wednesday."

"No surgery?"

"Never on a Wednesday." She sang it.

"Well that settles that."

"What do you mean?"

"Wednesday is the only day I'm free. No sense in making an appointment. Do all doctors take Wednesday off?"

"Thank God they do. I can catch up on my paperwork."

FROM THE back porch of the clubhouse Rosemary looked out over the golf course where the afternoon sun slanted through the trees and ignited the cream-colored carts darting hither and yon in pursuit of misdirected balls. Late April and you would think it was midsummer. Louis Poeglin was out there somewhere.

"He and his wife," Quinn told her in the pro shop. "They went out on the back nine an hour ago. If you want to catch up with them, head for fifteen."

Did she want to catch up with them? What for? Rosemary went into the bar and surprised herself by ordering a gin and tonic. It might have been a declaration that summer was here. At one table four men discussed the minutiae of their just-finished round. Two women in their sixties, all dressed up, faced one another at a small table, one hand gripping their drinks, the other flat on the table. Serious. Rosemary glanced at the two drinking women from time to time. They didn't say much to one another. They might have been herself and Beatrice.

Once they had spoken of living together in Beatrice's converted silo, but when Rosemary gave up her Minneapolis apartment and moved to Fairland it was into the house she had inherited from Stella. She had moved but she had not settled in. What prevented that was wondering about Stella.

There was no reason for Roy to deny he had killed her. Rosemary believed him when he said he didn't do it.

"Then who did?" Beatrice asked.

"Good question."

"The answer is Roy. Don't let him mislead you. You can't expect him to tell you he killed your aunt."

"It's not just me he won't tell."

"Sometimes I think you actually feel sorry for that creep."

She did. What if people thought she had killed Russ? What if people thought Beatrice had killed George? Beatrice did not like the analogies.

"Roy Hunt is still alive."

"Prison isn't much of a life."

"Good. Rosemary, he admits he killed George. He admits that he and Stella murdered George in cold blood. She paid. I think he escaped. He'll be paroled, you'll see."

"Not for years and years."

It was best not to discuss the matter with Beatrice. Rosemary told herself she would be equally cold-hearted if she thought Roy had killed Russ. She visited Roy again, probably a mistake, he seemed to think she had brought him news.

"All I think about, Rosemary, is that safe-deposit box."

His expression as he said that was agonized. George had put money in the box, the money was gone when Stella opened it, and then it was back when he showed the sheriff what had happened.

"Does it really matter?"

"Of course it matters!"

"Couldn't it have been George himself?"

He shook his head and smiled slyly. "I checked Phyllis's records. George Arthur never visited the vault after he put that money in the unregistered safe-deposit box."

"Stella herself?"

He shook his head. "Oscar Ewbank won't do anything about it, but I know who it was, Rosemary."

"Who?"

"Beatrice Dean!"

BEATRICE WAS not shocked to hear that Roy Hunt thought she had emptied and then filled the unregistered safe-deposit box.

"I did. George told me to when Roy and Stella suggested that he put money in an unregistered safe-deposit box. In a way, he had anticipated the idea by having me rent a box in my own name into which we began to put money in preparation for our departure.

But he pretended to go along with Roy's idea because he didn't want him wondering why he was accumulating so much cash. I had told George how careless Phyllis was with her ring of keys whenever I put money into the box I had rented, and that suggested the transfer. George put money into the unregistered box with great ceremony. Later he told me where the box was located and at the first opportunity, when Phyllis had left her keys and gone, I made the transfer to the box I rented in my name. George didn't intend to leave Stella anything he could carry away. Lock the door, will you?''

They were in Beatrice's office. It had been a week ago, on a Saturday morning. After the door was locked, Beatrice moved her chair back from the desk and pulled away a large piece of plastic that enabled her chair to roll more easily. Kneeling, Beatrice removed a section of the carpet. There was a sunken safe. She opened it, reached in and brought out a package of thousand-dollar bills.

"Good Lord."

Beatrice looked up at her. "This is yours too, Rosemary. All of it. Three and a half million dollars."

Rosemary took the package and sat in the chair Beatrice had pushed away from the desk. Beatrice sat on the floor and explained to Rosemary that the outstanding loans would be paid by those bidding for the company. All the banks and creditors would be satisfied. The purchasers would have a profitable company.

"It's the way George planned it, so no one would get hurt."

Rosemary did not understand. She did not want to understand. She gave the package to Beatrice, who fondled it a moment and then returned it to the floor safe.

"Stella never knew about that money? After George died?"

Beatrice gave her a look. "I would have burned it first."

The money had belonged to Stella after George was dead. If it was Rosemary's now, it was because she was Stella's heir.

She needn't have told me, Rosemary thought later. Beatrice could have taken all those millions of dollars and gone away, but she had stayed on to negotiate the sale of Arthur Enterprises. Once that money had represented a new life with George. Now that it no longer did, Beatrice did not covet it. But she would have done anything to keep it out of Stella's hands. That is why the safe-deposit box had been emptied too.

ROSEMARY WAS still in the clubhouse bar when the Poeglins came in, having finished nine holes. Babs sat right down at her table and flagged the bartender.

"What are you drinking, Rosemary?"

Louis did not sit down. "I gather you don't want to play the back nine."

"I didn't want to play the front nine." Babs gave Rosemary a look.

"Then I will leave you." He actually bowed.

"Louis belongs in the nineteenth century. Or the Middle Ages. Whenever it was they had chastity belts."

Babs's effort to be worldly was comic. Rosemary, remembering what she had heard of Babs at the Erickson auction, repressed a smile.

"I miss Stella, Rosemary. I really do. Know why?"

"Tell me."

A Bloody Mary arrived and Babs attended to it first. "Stella and I were planning a New York trip. Just the two of us. Stay in a nice hotel, go to a few shows, just *play.*"

How pathetic this middle-aged hope that happiness is misbehaving.

"Would *you* like to go to New York?"

"I hate New York."

Babs made a face. "That's right. You even prefer Fairland to Minneapolis."

"Claudia Cartwright called on me."

"Claudia's all right."

"That's what she told me."

Babs laughed, her eyes on the table of four men. "Well, I hate to drink and run."

"Where are the two of you going?"

"I don't know where Louis is going. I'm going to have lunch with Mabel Nicodemus. Maybe I can convince her to go to New York with me."

"How about Claudia?"

"It may come to that."

ROSEMARY ASKED to have her car brought, and when it came up the drive Louis Poeglin was at the wheel. He stopped and leaned across to open the passenger door.

"I'd like to talk with you," he said with a toothy smile.

She got in. "Talk?"

"Buckle up."

She did and he shot down the drive, throwing her back against the seat. He did not go through the gates but took a left onto a service road that led to the maintenance buildings and beyond to a vague track along the inside of the fence.

"Where are you going?"

"Miss Mulvaney tells me you have been at my office."

"Yes?"

"Checking up on me." A fleeting glance and again the toothy smile, but then he concentrated on his driving. To their left was the third fairway. It was difficult to feel alarm in this familiar daytime setting.

"You said you were in surgery the day Stella was killed."

"And you've learned that wasn't true."

"Miss Mulvaney says you were at the building site of your new clinic."

"Do you believe her?" He had slowed as he entered the woods along the seventh fairway.

"Why shouldn't I? Where were you?"

"I think you know."

Her hand moved toward the clasp of her seat belt. She wished she had not put it on. She must unsnap it, push the button that unlocked the door, open it . . . How complicated it seemed to get out of a car. Louis stopped the car now. Ahead there was a large metal building that seemed vaguely familiar. Rosemary pressed the release of her seat belt. The click was like a gunshot in the quiet car. His hand closed on her wrist.

"You've seen what Babs is like. I hold your aunt at least partly responsible for that. There are others. Babs wants to go off to New York without me and have fun!" He was squeezing her wrist now.

"She told me."

"She thinks you'll go with her."

"I won't."

"No," he said. "No, you won't."

"Did you kill Stella?"

He turned and looked directly at her. "She was a tramp. She'd been carrying on with Roy Hunt for years. It came out at the trial. Imagine that! Babs and I bumped into them once in Minneapolis. Their guilty expressions told it all. Babs was fascinated. After that she started to talk about going to New York. I'm no fool."

"You're hurting my wrist."

He ignored her. "She made a fool of herself in Minneapolis. Chasing after Nicodemus, that's what she was doing."

"Nicodemus!"

"Once I thought if only Claudia was gone, it would be different. I changed my mind. Stella was the main problem."

"So you killed her."

He angled her elbow and pulled her toward him. His expression grew calm.

"No one else knows. What made you think so?"

"You said you were in surgery."

"Ah." With his free hand he took her seat belt and tried to loop it over her head. Rosemary bent and sank her teeth into his wrist, deep, feeling the flesh break way, hearing his scream. Her hand was free, she pushed the unlock button but before she could get the door open he locked it again, using the panel on the driver's door. His wrist was bleeding freely where she had bitten him. He was no longer calm. When he tried again to loop the seat belt over her head, Rosemary pressed on the horn, holding it down despite his efforts to pry her hand from the wheel.

She held on for a minute but then he began to choke her, forcing her back against her locked door. His expression now was that of a technician at work. She felt his thumbs move on her throat and then he pressed and she gagged as her air was cut off. She was flailing her arms and kicking, hurting herself, trying to get free, as the world began to dissolve. Just before it went black she saw a bald, bearded face over Louis Poeglin's shoulder and then there was the crash of glass.

Gasping, drinking in lungfuls of sweet air, Rosemary became aware of Steve Nicodemus dragging Louis out of the car and subduing him.

TWENTY-FOUR

STEVE NICODEMUS had always relied on word of mouth for people to learn of the bookstore, but the hullabaloo that followed his stopping Louis Poeglin from killing Rosemary was a mixed blessing. Scruffy youths came to inquire about comic books, furtive men asked where the adult section was, women seemed to want to get a look at the man the Fairland *Tribune* had called a hero.

"Isn't a hero a fat sandwich?" Mabel asked.

"Sort of like a fat lip."

"You're supposed to save women, not threaten them."

"You're no woman, you're my wife."

Good old Mabel. Actually, she was the one who had heard the car horn back there in the woods and told him to see what was going on. Steve didn't like to think what might have happened if he hadn't found the rock he used to break the window.

"I can't imagine him killing Stella Arthur," Mabel said.

"I can."

"You never liked her."

"I meant I can imagine it. He would have killed Rosemary."

"If a hero hadn't arrived in time."

They were in the bookstore putting George Arthur's books into cartons for Rosemary. She was paying twelve thousand for them. She would have paid fifteen if he'd let her. Rosemary was keeping the house in Fairland but selling off Arthur Enterprises. She would live in Minneapolis but come to Fairland regularly, even after Louis Poeglin's trial, where she would have to testify.

"Rosemary and Beatrice are buying condominiums in the same building in Minneapolis," Mabel said.

"Who told you?"

"Babs."

"When does she leave?"

"They catch the ship in Miami and cruise the Caribbean for three weeks."

"Cruising with Claudia Cartwright," he mused.

"In every sense of the term."

"You should have gone with them."

"Can't you just see me on a love boat?"

"Vaguely."

She threw a book at him. It came through the air, pages fluttering like bird wings, money falling from it like manna. Mabel scrambled after it, collecting the twenty-dollar bills that had been concealed in the book.

She looked at Steve in wonderment. "Two hundred and twenty dollars!"

He just stood there looking at her.

"Steve, what should we do with it?"

He picked up the fallen book and handed it to her.

"Put the money back in the goddamn book and pack it!"

HUGH PENTECOST
WITH INTENT TO KILL

MURDER CHECKS IN...

Murder is an unwelcome spotlight on Pierre Chambrun's beloved
hotel. All the more unwelcome when the mutilated body is that of a
fifteen-year-old boy and when the mystery further involves a pop
idol, a brutally beaten centerfold, a soft-porn king, a religious
zealot, an employee found dead in a laundry hamper and another
with a concussion.

It's a convoluted case worthy of the dapper Chambrun. But time is
running out as the murderer readies to strike again.

"Suspenseful with a surprise ending."

— *Clarion Ledger/Daily News*

MURDER AT MUSKET BEACH

BERNIE LEE

TONY PRATT WAS TIRED OF HIDING BODIES

Then the popular mystery writer and his wife, Pat, found a corpse in their own backyard—and suddenly, murder wasn't so black-and-white anymore. Now it was bloodred...and very real.

Carl Conley, hotshot local Realtor, part-time mayor and small-time actor, is found dead as driftwood on the sand of Musket Beach, a tourist town on the Oregon Coast.

With an ear for dialogue, a nose for trouble and a habit for murder, Tony and Pat do some sleuthing of their own. Locking horns with the local law, they find themselves caught in the intrigue of a million-dollar deal gone sour, illicit love gone bad and a desperate killer waiting to strike again.

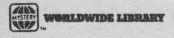

MYSTERY WORLDWIDE LIBRARY

DEADLY PROMISE
MIGNON F. BALLARD

You'd better watch out,
You'd better not cry,
Or there's no doubt
You're the next one to die...

The first victim was her husband. Then his best friend. So Molly Stonehouse had come to Harmony, Georgia, for Christmas—to discover who in her husband's cheery hometown was a murderer.

At the center of the mystery is a secret from the past, an innocent, boyish prank that, decades later, is unfolding with deadly precision.

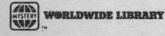

WORLDWIDE LIBRARY

HAL'S OWN MURDER CASE
LEE MARTIN

LABOR PAINS

Two weeks away from the birth of her baby, Ft. Worth detective
Deb Ralston decided her sixteen-year-old son, Hal, had picked a rotten
time to hitchhike halfway across the state with his girlfriend, Lorie, and be
arrested for murder.

The victim, a young woman, had been hacked with Hal's hunting knife
and left in Lorie's sleeping bag. Now Lorie is missing and Hal's in jail.

Ralston hits the tiny East Texas town in her official capacity as worried
mother—a role that quickly expands into investigating officer. The trail
leads to places of the heart no mother-to-be wants to go...but with a cop's
unerring instinct, she follows the ugly path into the twisted mind of a
ruthless killer.

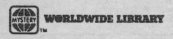

Can you keep a secret?

You can keep this one plus 2 free novels.